Praise for
SAMMY KEYES AND THE HOTEL THIEF

"Sammy's smart-mouthed and hard-hitting, unpopular at school and on the outs with the law. Readers follow the sleuth through her saucy first-person narrative…[which] delights from start to finish. This young gumshoe is certainly worth watching. Keep your binoculars trained on Sammy Keyes."
—*Publishers Weekly*

"Van Draanen debuts a live-wire young sleuth in this nonstop whodunit. Children will admire Sammy's inadvertent genius for ruffling feathers as much as they'll like her sharp powers of observation and deduction."
—*Kirkus Reviews*

"If Kinsey Millhone ever hires a junior partner, Sammy Keyes will be the first candidate on the list."
—Sue Grafton,
author of *A Is for Alibi* through *N Is for Noose*

"This girl sleuth is no well-mannered Nancy Drew. She's endearingly hot-tempered, nosy and not always obedient—in short, she's someone I want to read about again."
—Margaret Maron,
author of *The Bootlegger's Daughter*

Also by Wendelin Van Draanen:

Sammy Keyes and the Skeleton Man

And coming soon:

Sammy Keyes and the Sisters of Mercy

sammy keyes

AND THE hotel thief

by WENDELIN VAN DRAANEN

SCHOLASTIC INC.

New York Toronto London Auckland Sydney
Mexico City New Delhi Hong Kong

ISBN 0-439-06505-4

Text copyright © 1998 by Wendelin Van Draanen Parsons.
Illustrations and cover art copyright © 1998 by Dan Yaccarino.
All rights reserved. Published by Scholastic Inc.,
555 Broadway, New York, NY 10012, by arrangement
with Alfred A. Knopf, Inc. SCHOLASTIC and associated logos
are trademarks and/or registered trademarks of Scholastic Inc.

12 11 10 9 8 7 6   0 1 2 3 4/0

Printed in the U.S.A.   40

First Scholastic printing, September 1999

To my husband, Mark Parsons,
who leads a not-so-secret life as my hero.

Special thanks to Nancy Siscoe for her vision
and follow-through, to Ed and Rosalyn Parsons
for being such angels with my cherubs,
and to Ginger Knowlton—"Yes!"

sammy keyes

AND THE hotel thief

PROLOGUE

Grams told me
my binoculars
were going to get me
into trouble.

I just didn't believe her. See, Grams worries. All the time. About the way I dress and the food I eat, about me getting home on time, and especially about nosy Mrs. Graybill seeing me come and go. It's not like I try to upset her—I try real hard not to—it's just that somehow Grams winds up worrying and I usually get blamed for it.

So when she'd see me looking out the window with my binoculars and say, "Samantha Keyes, you mark my words, those things are going to get you in a big heap of trouble someday," I'd just say, "Mmm," and keep right on looking. I figured it was just Grams doing some more worrying about nothing.

That is, until I saw a man stealing money from a hotel room across the street—and he saw me.

1

ONE

It's not like I was trying to get into trouble. And it's not like it was *my* fault I was stuck inside the apartment. If it was anybody's fault it was Mrs. Graybill's. Mrs. Graybill lives down the hall and has to be the nosiest person who ever lived. I swear she's got nothing better to do than to stand by her door, waiting for someone to do something she doesn't think they're supposed to be doing. Grams says she's just a bitter old woman, but when I ask *why* she's bitter, Grams doesn't seem to have much of an answer. She usually just shrugs and says, "It happens to people sometimes," and then changes the subject.

Anyhow, it's on account of Mrs. Graybill that I was stuck inside when I wanted to be outside. And since there's not much for me to do because everything I own has to be able to fit inside Grams' bottom dresser drawer, I was using the binoculars to at least see what was going on outside.

First I checked out the Pup Parlor. You can see some pretty weird-looking dogs leaving the Pup Parlor. Most of them come out all puffed up and wearing ribbons like they're going to a party instead of home to sleep on the couch. But since we're on the fifth floor and the Pup Parlor's clear down the street, there isn't really much to see if nobody's going in to pick up their puffy dogs. And since nobody *was* going in to pick up their puffy dogs, I didn't spend much time watching.

I didn't waste time at Bargain Books, either. The only interesting thing I ever saw there was when the owner, Mr. Bell, chased this kid all the way down to Main Street, yelling at the top of his lungs, "Stop! You come back here and get your filthy bubble gum off my wall!" His face was all red and I thought he was going to have a heart attack. He caught the guy in the middle of the intersection at Broadway and Main and dragged him clear back up to the bookstore by his collar. Then he made him pull the gum off the wall and throw it in a trash can. The boy looked really embarrassed, kind of checking around to see if anyone was watching him pick these big strands of goopy gum off the wall. I waved, but he didn't see me, and pretty soon Mr. Bell let him go.

Anyhow, I cruised right by the bookstore and started checking out the hotel. Grams hates the Heavenly Hotel—calls it seedy, but I think she's wrong. One time I even went inside. There was a man with greased-back hair sitting behind the counter reading a newspaper and smoking a cigar. He kind of eyed me from behind the paper, then rolled his cigar over to one side of his mouth and said, "Lookin' for someone?"

I just smiled and shook my head and sat down in one of the fuzzy green chairs they have waiting for you in the lobby. I'd always wanted to sit in a chair like that. The kind with the curvy legs that have paws on the ends of them and then backs that go way up. The backs on the ones in the Heavenly Hotel are pointy—like the pope's hat, only green.

Anyhow, I'm busy trying out one of the chairs when the guy behind the counter says, "You sure?"

I nod and ask him, "How old do you have to be to live here?"

He squints at me and rolls his cigar from one side of his mouth to the other. "Where's your mother?"

Now there's no way I wanted to get into *that*, so I just hopped out of the chair and headed for the door. I'd seen about enough of the Heavenly Hotel anyways. It wasn't anything like Grams had told me. I was expecting a bunch of people hanging around like they do in front of the Salvation Army but all I got to see was some old guy gnawing on a cigar.

Anyhow, from our window you can't see the pope-hat chairs or the guy with the cigar—not even with binoculars. Actually, you can't see much of anything until you're looking at about the third floor. Then things start getting pretty good. Usually you just see people looking out their windows, pointing to stuff on the street or talking on the phone, but sometimes you can see people yelling at each other, which is really strange because you can't *hear* anything.

So I'd started looking at the hotel windows and was checking out the fourth floor when I noticed this guy moving around one of the rooms kind of fast. He disappeared for a little while but when he came back by the window I could see him digging through a purse like a dog after a gopher. And not only was he pawing through a purse, he was wearing gloves. Black gloves.

5

What I should've done was put those binoculars down and call 911. What I did instead was try to get the focus tight on my right eye. When I got the binoculars adjusted so that I could practically see him breathing in and out, I got the strangest feeling that I'd seen this guy before. Either that, or I knew his brother or something.

And I'm trying to get a better look at his face through all his bushy brown hair and beard, when he stuffs a wad of money from the purse into his jacket pocket and then looks up. Right at me.

For a second there I don't think he believed his eyes. He kind of leaned into the window and stared, and I stared right back through the binoculars. Then I did something really, really stupid. I waved.

He didn't wave back. He just took a good hard look at me and then ducked out of view.

I sat there for a minute not knowing what to do. I wanted to run and tell Grams, but I knew all *that* would do was get me in trouble. See, she doesn't know I look at the hotel—she thinks I just watch people on the street. Besides, I'd have to tell her about how he saw me, and that would make her worry. *I* was worried, and if I was worried you can just picture how Grams would be.

I thought about dialing 911, but the only phone in the apartment is in the kitchen and since Grams was in there making dinner I couldn't exactly go dialing Emergency without her knowing about it.

Then I thought about running down to the police station. It's only about four blocks from the apartment and I could've been there in no time. Trouble was, Mrs. Graybill.

So I'm sitting there, trying to figure out what to do, when Grams calls, "Samantha? It's time to feed that cat of yours."

I jumped right up and said, "Coming!" and the whole time I'm fixing Dorito's dinner, I'm watching Grams out of the corner of my eye.

Well, she's measuring out some rice, watching *me* out of the corner of *her* eye. Pretty soon she stops measuring. "What have you been up to, young lady?"

"Up to? Me?"

She puts down the measuring cup and takes off her glasses. "Yes, Samantha, you."

I check out my high-tops for a minute, kind of studying the place where the rubber's peeling away at the toe. "Nothing."

"Ha!" That's all she says. "Ha!" But what that *means* is I'm busted and had better start doing some pretty fast talking. Either that or come right out and tell the truth.

I step on the peeling rubber with my other foot, trying to break it off, but it just snaps back. When I look up at Grams, her hands have made it up to her hips so I know it's time to come out with the truth. At least part of it.

"I was using the binoculars. Sorry."

She lets out a little sigh—"Oh"—and turns back to the rice.

So there I am, waiting for her to ask me what I saw, thinking that maybe I'll tell her because I'm feeling kind of shaky about the whole thing, but she doesn't ask. She just sprinkles out some more rice and says, "Well, I suppose it can't be helped with Daisy being such a busybody today." And I'm standing there, not real sure I like getting off the hook so easy, when she turns to me and says, "You know what the problem is? The problem is that I haven't taught you how to knit."

I couldn't believe my ears. "To *knit?*"

Now Grams doesn't usually get too excited about stuff but when she does you can tell because her eyes get really big and she starts *moving.* And thinking about teaching me to knit was making those eyes of hers pop *wide* open. I just said, "Uh-oh," and got real busy giving Dorito fresh water.

It didn't help. She comes over to me with this measuring cup full of rice and says, "To knit, or crochet, or embroider—that's it! I'm going to teach you how to embroider."

"*Embroider?*" I fill up Dorito's water dish. "No way!"

She chases after me with that cup of rice in her hand. "It would be fun. Trust me, you would enjoy it! Besides, it would give you something constructive to do on the days when you have to stay in."

I look straight at her. "I would *hate* it." Then I point to the kettle of water splashing away like crazy on the stove. "Water's boiling."

She hurries over to the stove. "How do you know you'd hate it? You've never even tried it."

I laugh. "Oh yes I have. Lady Lana tried to teach me."

"*Please* don't call her that."

I just shrug. "Well she did. When I was in the third grade. I kept poking myself with the needle and she got mad at me 'cause I bled all over the place."

Grams didn't have much to say to that. I mean, everyone knows how much my mother likes blood. So she stirs the rice some and finally she says, "Well, okay then. I'll teach you how to knit."

I groan, but I can tell it's hopeless. Grams is going to teach me how to knit whether I like it or not.

Just then the doorbell rings. Now normally when the doorbell rings I just get up from doing whatever I'm doing, make sure none of my stuff is sitting around the living room, and head for Grams' closet.

This time, though, I jumped. I jumped and I yelped like a puppy. And all of a sudden my heart's pounding because I know who it is.

It's the guy I saw at the Heavenly Hotel, come to shut me up for good.

TWO

The only thing I could find in Grams' closet to use on the guy was an umbrella. It was one of the old kind, big and black with a nice fat point. I sat there, waiting, holding the thing like a spear. And when Grams finally opened the closet door, well, I was so sure it was the guy from the Heavenly that I almost jabbed her in the stomach.

She jumps back. "Samantha Jo! What in the world—?"

I peek around her and whisper, "Who was that?"

"It's Marissa." She yanks the umbrella away from me and puts it back in the closet.

"Marissa? What's she doing here?"

Grams just shrugs. "Go ask her yourself."

I go charging out to the living room and there's Marissa, kind of dancing around with her feet pointing toward each other, chewing on a fingernail. "What's wrong?"

She starts dancing even faster. "It's Mikey! We were playing video games at the mall and all of a sudden I turned around and he was gone. I can't find him any-where. Mom's supposed to be home in half an hour and if she finds out—"

"Okay, okay.... Did you check the pet store?"

She says, "The pet store!" like it's some brainstorm instead of the very first place she should've looked. "Come on!"

I yank on her sweatshirt. "Hang on, would you?" Then I go find Grams and say, "Would you check the hall?"

"But it's dinnertime!"

I look over at Marissa, who's chewing on a nail. "It's important, Grams."

She thinks about this for a minute, then sighs. "Well, okay." She peeks down at Mrs. Graybill's door and looks back with a smile. "Don't be long."

So we tiptoe past Mrs. Graybill's place, then race to the fire escape stairs.

Now I don't always use the fire escape stairs. Sometimes I use the regular stairs and sometimes I even use the elevator. It depends. The elevator's okay to use if I'm leaving and not coming back, like if I'm going to spend the night at Marissa's. The regular stairs I'd use all the time, only they come out right by the mailboxes and it seems like someone always sees me. With the fire escape all I have to worry about is that someone's going to notice the wad of gum I put in the jamb to keep it from locking, and so far no one has.

So we go banging down the stairs and pretty soon we're running past the Dumpsters, across the parking lot to Main Street, and over to the mall.

Since the pet store's way down at the far end of the mall we decide to first check for Mikey at the arcade, just in case *he's* looking for Marissa.

Mikey's kind of hard to miss. He's what Grams calls a little butterball. He's got curly black hair that never looks combed, even when it's just been combed. He's short, even for someone who's only eight years old, and fat.

Really fat. Mrs. McKenze says he'll grow out of it, but in the meantime he's stocking up on candy bars.

Anyhow, we check the arcade but he's not there, and as we're running toward the escalator I ask, "Did you have him paged?"

"Paged?"

I duck past people on the escalator. "Yeah, paged! You know, 'Mikey McKenze, please report to the arcade immediately. Your sister is looking for you.'"

She catches up to me. "You can do that?"

"Sure. People do it all the time."

Just then the mall loudspeakers blare, "Good afternoon, shoppers! This is Rockin' Rick comin' atcha from the KRQK rock party booth. We're set up right outside Jammin' Records on the south end of the first level, and we've been here all weekend giving away prizes. We've only got a few hours to go on this back-to-school weekend and we've still got mountains to give away. CDs, calculators, sweatshirts, a five-in-one Kanga book bag...you name it, we're trying to give it away. Stop by the booth and register! It's fast, it's free, and you still have time. That's the KRQK party booth, right outside Jammin' Records. Come on down!"

Marissa stops moving. "That was Rockin' Rick!"

I yank on her and say, "You're in a panic about Mikey, remember?"

"But that's Rockin' Rick! He's here!"

I pull her off the escalator. "So we'll meet him after we check the pet store. C'mon!"

We race down the mall and we're flying past Juicers

when Marissa squeaks to a stop. "Hey, look! My cousin's working! Maybe he's seen Mikey."

Brandon's a nice guy. He's in high school and he's on the swim team so his hair's turned this really shiny red where it used to be black. He's really friendly and even invites Marissa and me to his swim meets sometimes. Most kids in high school won't even talk to you if you're in junior high. They act like you're a baby or pretend you're not even there.

Anyhow, we run up to the counter and Marissa says, "Brandon! Have you seen Mikey? He was supposed to stick with me at the arcade and I don't know what happened—he took off."

Brandon smiles. "You can't miss Mikey." He points and says, "He was headed thataway—about twenty minutes ago." Then he says, "Hiya, Sammy. How's life?"

I don't know why, but whenever Brandon talks to me I wind up looking at my feet, not knowing what to say. So there I am, looking down, popping the rubber on my high-tops, and what do I say? "Fine." Brilliant, huh? Fine.

Marissa tugs on my arm and says to Brandon, "If you see him, tell him to go back to the arcade and wait for me, okay?"

Brandon waves and says, "Will do," and off we go to the pet store.

The pet store used to sell real pets. You know, like dogs? Now they only sell mice and birds and your occasional box turtle. Those and fish. Rows and rows of fish. I don't care what anyone says, fish don't belong in a pet store. They

13

are not pets. I could go my whole life without seeing another fish blubbing away in a tank.

Mikey couldn't. He can watch fish for hours. For a while there he kept asking the girl at the register if he could please feed the fish, but she always said no. I guess she was too busy reading her fashion magazine to be bothered making a roly-poly guy with chocolate all over his face happy. She told him they were on a schedule, if you can believe that.

Anyhow, we go charging into the pet store and there's the girl behind the register, reading a magazine. Marissa runs up and says, "Have you seen my brother?"

The girl just nods toward the fishtanks without even looking at us.

Mikey's there all right, sitting on the floor with a tub of popcorn, watching the fish go back and forth. Marissa hauls him to his feet. "You're supposed to stay with me!"

Popcorn goes flying everywhere, and Mikey's so surprised he starts choking. He tries to talk but you can't understand a word he's saying because he's too busy coughing.

Marissa shakes him. "Don't you ever do that again!"

Finally he spits out, "But you *said* I could!"

"I did not!"

Mikey wipes the popcorn off his face with the back of his hand and says real loud, "Did too!"

Marissa grabs him by the arm. "And look at all this stuff! You've had enough junk food to last you a year!"

"Have not!"

Marissa starts picking wrappers off the floor. "A Reese's,

a Snickers—no, *two* Snickers—an ice cream cone ..." She does a double take at the napkin and freezes. "You had a Double Dynamo!"

Mikey looks from side to side like he's about to bolt.

"You were supposed to stick with me and you went clear out to Maynard's?"

Mikey looks straight at her. "I didn't, honest! Oscar had his ice cream cart right outside Jammin' Records. I barely even had to go outside."

Marissa squints at him a minute, thinking. Finally she finishes picking up his mess and says, "Did you see the KRQK booth?"

Mikey shrugs. "Yeah."

"Did you see Rockin' Rick?"

Mikey shrugs again. "I think."

"Well? What did he look like?"

"I don't know...kinda dumb."

"Dumb? What do you mean, 'Kinda dumb'? Rockin' Rick's the coolest!" She turns to me and rolls her eyes. "Let's go down there and see if we can meet him."

So off we all go, down the escalator and over to the KRQK booth. There's music playing all right, and there are two ladies in the booth helping people register, but there's nobody who looks like he could be Rockin' Rick.

Marissa finally goes up and asks, and one of the ladies says, "He should be back in a little bit. Maybe twenty minutes?"

Marissa makes a face. "Darn! I can't wait that long. I've got to get home."

"Me too. Grams is probably holding dinner for me."

"Hey, you want to meet me on the steps at school tomorrow?" She laughs. "I get nervous just thinking about it!"

I say, "Sure!" because about the last thing I feel like doing is swimming through a sea of seventh- and eighth-graders all by myself.

I wave good-bye and head across the mall. And I'm busy thinking about what seventh grade is going to be like, when for some reason I look back over my shoulder. Then I look again, because coming straight at me is a man with bushy brown hair and a beard.

My heart about shoots through my chest, and the next thing you know I'm running. I race down the main corridor and then take a quick left and duck into the bookstore.

And I'm squatting down by the newspapers, peeking out the window, when here he comes, walking by. And I'm trying to figure out if he's the hotel thief or not, when all of a sudden he stops. Right in front of the bookstore.

My heart's whacking its way out of my chest and my legs are feeling really wobbly, but then the next thing you know he's kissing this lady and the two of them walk off, pushing their baby stroller.

I stayed in the bookstore a minute, trying to quit shaking, and when I finally caught my breath, I got up and started hurrying home.

And I guess I was still worrying about who was behind me because I kept looking over my shoulder, and when I turned a corner I bumped right into a man saddled up with shopping bags.

I said, "I'm sorry!" but he didn't say a word. He just pulled down the bill of his ball cap, picked up his packages, and walked away with his eyes to the ground.

I watched him go, and when he was out of sight I kind of shook my head and headed out of the mall.

And I was just thinking that I'd be back before Grams had had a chance to finish fluffing the rice, when I noticed police cars parked out in front of the Heavenly Hotel.

And with all the commotion at the hotel—well, there was no way I could just pass by without taking a peek inside.

THREE

I really thought it might only take a minute and that Grams wouldn't even notice I was late. I thought wrong. There were kids hanging around outside the Heavenly Hotel, peeking in the windows, but they didn't seem to know anything. And since the door was propped open, I just walked right in.

There were only adults inside, so I found a spot where I thought the policemen wouldn't notice me—right behind one of those pope-hat chairs.

Now I don't mind policemen. Actually, when I was in the fourth grade I wanted to *be* one, but that was before Lady Lana left me with Grams and I had to start worrying about someone finding out. When you're living where you're not supposed to be living, it doesn't take long to figure out that you should stay away from people who ask nosy questions, and believe me, policemen like to ask lots of nosy questions.

And you could tell they'd been asking this one lady lots and *lots* of nosy questions. The lady was wearing a dress that looked like it was made out of metal. It had tiny silver hoops all linked together that kind of shimmered when she moved. She had on pointy silver high heels and silver nylons, and she had really long fingernails that were painted black with silver moons and stars. Her hair was all swirled around on top of her head and plastered with so much hair spray that it didn't move, even though she was yelling and shaking her head back and forth so much that her long silver earrings were swinging around, practically hitting her in the cheeks.

I moved a little bit closer, behind another pope-hat chair. The policeman was telling her, "Now miss, please, calm down."

"Quit telling me to calm down! I'll calm down when you find my money!"

There are two policemen taking the report, but I can only see the face of one. He's tall and skinny and has lots of white teeth and a stringy little mustache. He says, "You say it was four thousand dollars?"

"What are you, deaf? Yes, four thousand dollars!"

The policeman scribbles away in his notebook. "And why did you say you were carrying this much cash around?"

Those earrings start flying again. "I *didn't* say, and it's none of your business! Your business is to find out who stole it from me!"

Tall 'n' Skinny just scribbles some more in his notebook, then tugs on a corner of his mustache and says, "We'll do our best."

She throws her hands up in the air. "That's *it*? That's all you're gonna do? What about fingerprints? Aren't you at least going to look for fingerprints?"

Before I can stop myself, I step out from behind the pope-hat chair and say, "You won't find any fingerprints."

For a second, everything's quiet. Tall 'n' Skinny quits

playing with his mustache, and the lady's earrings come in for a landing. Then everyone—and I mean *everyone*—turns around and stares at me. All of a sudden my throat's feeling kind of ticklish, so it only comes out as a whisper when I say, "He was wearing gloves."

The second policeman turns around to look at me, and I just want to disappear.

It's Officer Borsch, the man behind my one and only experience with the law. See, he gave me a ticket once. For jaywalking. And it's not like it's so bad, getting a ticket for jaywalking, it's just that I thought it was stupid. So I gave him the wrong name. The wrong name, and the wrong everything else.

So there I am, staring at him, trying like mad to remember the name I gave him when I got caught jaywalking. And I'm thinking that maybe I *shouldn't* remember it, because he's staring at me like he's trying to remember who I am, and if I give him the name I made up maybe he *will* remember, and then I'll be in some major trouble, when the lady croaks out, "What did you say?"

I mumble, "He was wearing gloves."

Officer Borsch says, "*Who* was wearing gloves?"

I try to shrink a few inches. "The man I saw on the fourth floor taking money out of a purse."

The lady yells, "See!"

Officer Borsch squints at me. "And how did you happen to see someone on the fourth floor stealing money out of a purse?"

Now you have to understand, Officer Borsch isn't the kind of man it's easy to lie to. He's big. He's Mikey, all grown up and in a very bad mood. His hair's done with Crisco, and his shirt is so tight it looks like he's trying to press it from the inside out. On top of that he's nosy. Very nosy. When he gave me that ticket for jaywalking, he must've asked me a hundred questions that didn't have a thing to do with jaywalking. And I thought I was so smart, answering every single one of them with a lie. I remember throwing the ticket away in a Dumpster, feeling like I'd just hit a home run, and now here I was—face to face with the Borsch-man, on the verge of getting thrown into Juvenile Hall.

"I asked you a question!"

"Huh? Oh! Ummmmmm..." I look around and can tell—everyone knows I'm trying to think up a lie. So I blurt out, "I saw him through binoculars."

"Binoculars?" he says. "From where?"

I try to sound real calm. "From across the street."

Officer Borsch squints even harder. "You want to tell me you could see someone clear up on the fourth floor from across the street?"

I nod and he blows air out of his mouth like a deflating balloon.

"Leave her alone!" The lady moves in a little closer to me. "Go ahead, honey, tell me what you saw."

I look at her for a minute, thinking that four thousand dollars is an awful lot of money and that if it were mine, I sure would want it back. Finally I say, "I was visiting my grandmother in the Senior Highrise. I was bored, so I started looking around with binoculars and I saw some guy taking money out of a purse."

She grabs me by the shoulders and I can feel her little fingernail galaxies digging into my back. "When? When did you see this?"

"About an hour ago."

She yells at Tall 'n' Skinny, "What did I tell you?" then turns back to me. "And honey, what did this man look like?"

"He had brown hair and a brown beard, and he was wearing black gloves and a black jacket."

Officer Borsch pushes the lady aside. "Was he tall, was he short?"

"Kind of medium."

"What kind of jacket was it?"

"It was straight with big pockets."

"What do you mean, 'straight'?" he asks.

"You know—it wasn't puffy, it was straight."

"Heavy?"

"Kind of medium."

He shakes his head. "'Kind of medium'—oh that's a real good description."

Well, let me tell you, I didn't like the way he was rolling his eyes and talking down to me. He was treating me like a stupid little kid, and I'm not a stupid little kid. So when he sighs and says, "Could you at least tell me, was he skinny or fat?" I point to Tall 'n' Skinny and say, "Well, he wasn't as skinny as him..." then I point to the Borsch-man, "...and he sure wasn't as fat as you."

The lady just busts up, but Officer Borsch doesn't think it's too funny. His neck gets kind of red and he puts his face right next to mine. "Look, little girl, we've had five burglaries in this vicinity in the past two weeks. We don't have time for your wisecracks. If you know something, tell us. If you don't, or if you're just making all this up, then go home to your mommy and let us do our work."

The lady steps in. "Honey, how old do you think he was?"

Now I'm okay at guessing some things, but age is not one of them. "I don't know, maybe . . . forty?"

Officer Borsch mumbles, "Kind of medium, huh?" and then laughs like he's the funniest guy in the building. He clears his throat. "Look, we'll get your name and number and if we have any further questions we'll just call you."

There goes my heart again, knocking away in my chest. "I've told you everything I can think of." Except, I'm thinking, the fact that it feels like I've seen the guy somewhere before.

Tall 'n' Skinny flips open his notebook. "Well, just in case, let's get your name and address."

Great. And I'm thinking, How do I get myself into these things? when out of my mouth pops, "Samantha Keyes, six three seven five East Jasmine."

Now if they were thinking at all, they would've taken one look at me and known—there's no way I live on East Jasmine. East Jasmine is where they have two houses to a block. East Jasmine is where they have gates in front of their driveways and riding mowers for their lawns. East Jasmine is where people from out of town go just to gawk.

And 6375 East Jasmine is where Marissa lives.

Tall 'n' Skinny doesn't even blink. He just scribbles it down and says, "Very good. We'll contact you if we need you."

So I say to the lady, "I hope you get your money back," and then head out the door.

One of the kids outside calls, "Hey, what's going on in there?"

I shrug, "Just a burglary." And I'm about to jaywalk across the street when I glance back at the Heavenly and see Officer Borsch watching me through the doorway.

I stop and head down to the intersection, because I can tell—Officer Borsch is not going to sleep well until he remembers just exactly where he's run into me before.

FOUR

Grams was mad all right. She made me eat cold fish and rice, and wouldn't let me get up from the table until I'd eaten every single cold pea rolling around on my plate. Normally I would've just slipped Dorito some of the fish and shoved the peas in my napkin, but Grams sat right across from me and I knew from the way she wasn't saying anything that it was a bad time to get caught using Dorito as a garbage disposal. On top of that, while I was choking down cold food she ate every last crumb of a big piece of pound cake. When I finished my dinner and asked for some, all she said was, "It's time for you to go to bed."

So I headed for the couch. The couch is actually pretty comfortable, and it beats sleeping on the floor or with Grams. I tried sleeping with Grams when I first moved in because I was having so many bad dreams. Trouble is, she snores so loud that I wasn't getting any sleep, so I finally started using the couch. I still get bad dreams once in a while, so sometimes I go in and listen to Grams snore, but most of the time the couch and I get along just fine.

And you might think that I'd have bad dreams after waving at the guy in the Heavenly Hotel and running into Officer Borsch, but I didn't. I slept like a log. I might even have snored.

In the morning when I woke up I thought about everything that had happened, and decided there was no way the guy at the Heavenly Hotel could know who I was. With those binoculars in front of my face and my hair pulled back in a ponytail like it was, I could've been anyone. He might even have thought I was an old person. I mean, if he knew anything about my Grams' building, that's what he'd think.

So there I was, lying on the couch, feeling pretty good, when the phone rings. Grams comes scooting out of her room in her robe and slippers and picks it up, and I can tell from the way she's talking that it's Lady Lana on the other end. So much for feeling good. After about five minutes of keeping her voice down, Grams covers up the phone and says, "Samantha, it's your mother. She'd really like to talk to you."

Normally I would've given Grams an argument, but seeing how I'd upset her so much the night before, I just went into the kitchen and took the phone.

Lady Lana starts gushing about how much she loves me and misses me and how she can't wait to see me again, but she's *so* close to landing a part in a major motion picture and has to stay just a little while longer. And the whole time she's talking I'm thinking that it's been over a year since she dumped me with Grams and told me she'd be back "soon." I really wanted to hang up on her like I usually do, but that upsets Grams, so I just stood there, counting the loops in the phone cord, not saying much.

When Lady Lana finally got off the phone, I went back to the couch and sat with the blanket wrapped all around me. Grams sits beside me and says real quiet, "I'm sorry about last night."

"Me too."

After a minute, she sighs. "You know your mother means well..."

"I just want to forget about her, okay?"

Grams is quiet for a little while, then perks up and says, "Say! It's your first day of junior high school—how about French toast for breakfast?"

I say, "Sure!" and while I'm getting ready for school Grams makes me French toast out of *pound cake*. It was the best French toast I'd ever had, and by the time I left for school I'd forgotten all about Lady Lana's phone call. Well, almost anyway.

*   *   *

Marissa was already waiting at the top of the school steps. I waved at her and ran up to meet her.

She pulls me aside and whispers, "This place is a zoo! I can't believe how many people are here."

We stand there a minute, watching everyone talking and laughing and moving like they know where they're going. Finally I look at Marissa and say, "Wow..."

"I know! And I don't see anybody I recognize, do you?"

I shake my head. "Maybe we should go find our homeroom."

We pull out our schedules and Marissa says, "B-2. I don't even remember where the B block is, do you?"

I didn't. Everything looked completely different when

we'd come down to check it out on our own. There hadn't been any *people*.

So we walked around in circles for a while and finally I said, "I haven't got a clue. Let's just ask someone, okay?"

Out of all the people walking around William Rose Junior High School that day, Marissa picks a girl with hair the color of fire and says, "Let's go ask her."

The girl looked like an eighth-grader, and from the way she was talking with the guy standing next to her, she seemed real comfortable being in a tidal wave of students. So Marissa was right—she probably knew exactly where B-2 was. I just would never have picked her because she looked, well, snotty. Partly it was the color she'd dyed her hair. Partly it was the earrings—she had five studs in each ear and a group of rings looped over the tops. Mostly, though, it was the way she looked at us when we walked over. Like we were kicking sand in her corner of the beach.

I almost grabbed Marissa and suggested we find someone else, but before I knew it she was saying, "Excuse me. Do either of you know where B-2 is?"

At first Firehead just snubs us, but then she notices my shoes. And she laughs. "High-tops? What are you, straight from elementary school?"

I stare at her a minute and can feel my face getting really hot. How can someone who decorates her ears like a Christmas tree have the nerve to make fun of my high-tops? And I'm about to tell her to keep her snotty thoughts to herself when the guy she's standing next to says, "Hey...aren't you Brandon McKenze's cousin?"

Marissa smiles at him. "Yeah, I am. Who are you?"

"I'm Taylor Briggs. My brother and him are best friends. You don't remember me? I was at his pool party this summer."

Marissa blinks a bit, then says, "Sorry, there were so many people there..."

"That's all right." He takes her schedule and says, "What room are you looking for?"

"B-2. It's our homeroom."

Now while Taylor's talking to Marissa, Firehead's getting real roasty around the collar. And when he's done telling us how to get to B-2, she glares at us, then throws her nose in the air and goes back to talking to Taylor.

When we're far enough away I say, "Wow! She was scary!"

Marissa laughs. "You're not kidding!" And we hurry off to find B-2.

Our homeroom teacher, Mrs. Ambler, was already in the classroom, rearranging things on her desk. The bell rings and she looks up at the clock, then smiles at us and says, "We still have one more bell. Go ahead and find yourselves seats."

We find a couple of seats near the back, and I say to Marissa, "I've been wanting to tell you about what happened yesterday."

Marissa checks out the people around her. "Oh yeah? What?"

Kids are piling into the classroom, and since I don't want anyone else to hear, I whisper, "You know the Heavenly Hotel?"

Just then the tardy bell rings and Mrs. Ambler calls, "Find a desk. You'll have assigned seats by the end of the week, but for now sit where you like."

So we're looking around at everyone scrambling for a seat near the back, when who walks in the door? Firehead.

I nudge Marissa. "Look!"

At first I thought she was there to deliver a message or something, but when she sits at a desk kitty-corner from me it hits me—she's no snot-nosed eighth-grader. She's a snot-nosed seventh-grader.

I must have been staring, because she turns around and says, "What are you looking at?" Then she eyes my shoes and says, "You freak."

Mrs. Ambler calls, "Settle down, class. Let's begin." And as she's welcoming us to our first day of junior high school, explaining the rules for homeroom, Firehead leans back and says, "Taylor says you look like a fourth-grader."

Now maybe I'm kind of skinny and maybe I don't wear makeup or get all decked out to go to school, but there's no way I look like I'm in the fourth grade.

Mrs. Ambler asks the class to stand so we can pledge the flag, so I stand up and say, "Bug off, would you?"

Firehead pulls a face like Oh, I'm so scared and then leans over again and says, "Whatcha gonna do? Kick me with a high-top?" She puts her hand in front of her mouth. "Ooooh...I'm petrified!"

I roll my eyes and keep on pledging, but I'm thinking, What's your *problem*?

Now Firehead's not saying the Pledge. She's got her

hand on her heart but her eye on me. And when we're just about done, she leans back and says, "Oh, you say the Pledge so *good*. Did you spend the summer practicing?"

Mrs. Ambler looks straight at her. "Young lady, what is your name?"

Firehead looks around a bit, then points to herself and asks, "Me?"

Mrs. Ambler snaps, "Yes, you."

She gives her an innocent little look. "Heather. Heather Acosta."

"Well, Miss Acosta, maybe your elementary school teachers allowed you to talk during the Pledge, but you're in junior high school now and we expect a degree of maturity from you. I'd like to try it again, only this time I'd like you to come up here and lead us."

All of a sudden homeroom is dead quiet. And while everyone's busy thinking there's no way they're *ever* going to talk during the Pledge in Mrs. Ambler's class, Heather's eyes move from side to side like she doesn't quite believe what's happening to her.

Finally she moves to the front of the class, and by the time she's done leading the Pledge, her face is as red as her hair. And when she gets back to her chair she gives me the wickedest evil eye I've ever seen, and I can tell she's thinking that somehow this is all *my* fault.

I can also tell that Heather Acosta is going to find a way to get me back. And when she does, it'll be in spades.

FIVE

The morning took forever. Ms. Pilson sat us in alphabetical order and then spent the rest of the period giving us "a taste of things to come" in her English class. She read poems in Old English, which was like listening to someone read in Greek or Russian.

In math, Mr. Tiller sat us in alphabetical order and then tried to get us fired up about the "concept of variables." We all just kind of stared while he and X danced around the chalkboard.

In history, Mr. Holgartner thought he'd be real tricky and sat us in *reverse* alphabetical order. Then he told us we'd be watching a lot of films in his class and proceeded to pop in a video of an ancient black-and-white movie about settlers of the West. It might have been an okay film, but the narrator's voice kept warbling around and the tracking kept going off. I wanted to put my head down, but Mr. Holgartner was working on something right next to me, so I had to sit there and pretend to be interested.

When lunchtime finally rolled around, I was already tired of being in junior high.

Marissa ran to get a hot lunch while I staked out a table on the patio. When she finally came back, she unwrapped her hamburger and said, "So what were you trying to tell me in homeroom this morning?"

I take a bite of my peanut-butter-and-jelly sandwich and say, "You're not going to believe what happened yesterday—" Then I see Heather heading straight for our table. I nudge Marissa with my foot. "Uh-oh. Here comes Scarlett O'Hair."

"Who?" Marissa turns around to see, then whispers, "She's not coming over *here*, is she?"

Well, sure enough, Heather sits down, right next to Marissa.

Marissa dips a French fry into her catsup and tries to ignore her.

Heather says, "Hey, that looks really good. Can I have some?"

Now the hamburger and fries do not look good. They look shriveled-up and greasy. Marissa looks at her and says, "Where's your lunch?"

Heather lets out a pathetic little sigh. "Mom sent me to school with no lunch money. She wanted me to brown-bag it." She looks at me. "Like I want to be associated with nerds who do that."

I pull an apple out of my lunch sack. "Why don't you go ask one of your friends for a loan?"

Heather gives me this catty little smile, then does something really weird—she moves over to *my* side of the table, gets right in my face, and says, "Was I talking to you?"

I stare right back at her. "Maybe not, but I'm talking to you. You don't even know us and you're trying to mooch food?"

She gives me that smile again, then says to Marissa, "I just need a few bucks for lunch. C'mon, you can afford it."

Marissa looks at me and what she's thinking is, Oh no! Not already! Because when we were in the sixth grade everyone was always asking her for money, and she could never just tell them to get lost.

Marissa whispers, "Taylor."

Heather smiles and says, "Yeah. He tells me you're loaded."

I say, "Just bug off, would you?"

Well Heather doesn't bug off. What she does is she gives me another catty little smile; then she sticks me in the butt with a pin.

I yelp and jump about three feet off the bench. Heather laughs, and as she's leaving she says to Marissa, "You gotta dump the deadweight if you want to get anywhere around here."

For a second there my mouth is hanging wide open, and I'm dancing around because my butt is *burning* and I can't believe what's just happened.

Marissa glances over her shoulder at Heather and then back at me. "What happened? Sammy, what did she *do*?"

Well, my heart's pounding and my palms are starting to get all sweaty, and before I can stop myself I'm off the bench, chasing after Heather. I push through a crowd of people and when I get up to her I turn her around by the shoulder and punch her. Right in the nose.

Blood gushes all over the place and she starts screaming at the top of her lungs. And what do I do? I walk right back to our table and take a great big bite of peanut butter and jelly.

Heather's across the patio, screaming like crazy, and there's a bunch of kids around her trying to get a better look at all the blood running down her face. Marissa says, "What happened?"

"She stuck me in the butt with a pin so I punched her in the nose."

Marissa's eyes bug right out. "You did *what?*"

"I punched her in the nose."

Marissa's still dumbfounded and I'm still gnashing away on my peanut butter and jelly when this man in a suit and a scuba watch shows up. He says, "The kids tell me you're the one who punched Heather in the nose. Is that right?"

Now the man looks like he could be a professional wrestler if he'd let his hair grow out and get a suntan. And it seems kind of dangerous lying to him, so I swallow the last bite of sandwich, then nod and say, "That's right. But I only did it because she stuck me in the butt with a pin."

"Mmm-hmm. Come with me."

As he's marching me away from the patio, I look over my shoulder and ask, "What about Heather?"

"The nurse is attending to her. I'll have a talk with her when I'm done with you."

So I follow him to an office with a big brass plaque on the door that reads: MR. CAAN, VICE PRINCIPAL. We go inside and it's finally dawning on me that I'm in some pretty serious trouble.

Mr. Caan sits me down and tells me how nobody saw Heather do anything to me but that everybody saw me pop her in the nose. He lectures me about maturity and "brawling" on his campus, and when he finally asks me if

I have anything to say for myself, I say, "Yes!" and tell him how Heather's been picking on me the whole day. And when I'm finally done and he's still looking like he doesn't believe me, I stand up and offer to show him the spot where Heather tattooed me.

He stutters a minute and winds up saying no, that won't be necessary. Then he hurries me out of his office, straight to the Box.

The Box is a room that's even smaller than Grams' closet. It's got nothing on the walls but paint, nothing but a light on the ceiling, and in the middle of all that nothingness is a rusty metal chair. That's it. Basically it's just a big box where they stick you when you've been bad.

Mr. Caan didn't call it the Box, though. He called it the Reflection Room. What he said was, "Samantha, I think you should spend a little time in our Reflection Room thinking about what you've done today. Spend some time reflecting on why hitting Heather was not a good solution to your problem with her." When I stepped inside he said, "I'll be back for you in a little while," and then closed the door tight.

I spent some time looking around at the cinder-block walls, wondering how in the world I could've gotten into so much trouble on my first day of junior high. Then I started thinking about Heather. I mean sure, I'd punched her in the nose, but I wasn't the one who'd started it. Why was I "reflecting" in the Box when Heather was out roaming around? And what kind of lies was she out there telling about me? And why did they believe her and not me?

The longer I sat there, the more positive I was that a punch in the nose was exactly what Heather Acosta had coming to her. I decided that if it ever happened again I'd punch that snotty little nose of hers all right, only this time I'd do it twice.

When Mr. Caan finally came back he stood there, kind of tapping the face of his watch. Finally he says, "Samantha, I'd like you to come back to my office for a few minutes. There are some things I'd like to discuss with you."

So I follow him to his office, thinking that it's going to be really hard for me to tell him I'm sorry about hitting Heather when I'm not.

Trouble is, he doesn't ask me anything about Heather or the punch in the nose. What he does is sit me down in his office and say, "Samantha, I just got off the phone from a very strange conversation…"

All of a sudden I really *am* sorry that I punched Heather in the nose. All of a sudden I'm feeling kind of sick to my stomach, wishing I could go back in time and take it all back. I know exactly what he's going to say. It's all over— Grams couldn't take it anymore and wound up telling him everything.

But what comes out of his mouth is "…with your mother."

"With my…mother?" I say, and then for once in my life I shut up. I mean, did he think Grams was my mom? Did he get Grams to give him my mother's number in Hollywood? Did Grams pretend to be my mom? I didn't know what to think. Grams had told me that if anyone ever called the apartment looking for my mom she would just tell them she was taking care of me while my mother was visiting her sick sister. My aunt Veronica...or was it Victoria? I can't remember. Lady Lana doesn't *have* a sister, so it doesn't really matter; it's just that that's what Grams told me she would do. And since Mr. Caan was sitting there behind his desk playing with his diving watch, not saying a word about anyone's sick sister, I didn't know what to think.

He studies the band of his watch. "Yes, Samantha, your mother. She sounded a bit...odd. Is she ill?"

Ill? How am I supposed to know? I don't even know who he talked to. I look down. "Ummm...some days are better than others."

He "hmmm"s and "uh"s for a minute and then finally says, "Is it serious?"

"Well...she doesn't really like to talk about it."

"I see." He goes back to studying his watch. Finally he says, "What do you suppose she had to say about what happened here today?"

I look down at my high-tops and say, "It depends. Did you tell her about Heather sticking me with a pin? Or"— I look up at him—"did you only tell her about me hitting her in the nose?"

He just sits there playing with his watch some more, so I plow right ahead. "Besides, I didn't even hit her that hard—"

He looks straight at me. "Young lady, Heather was in such pain that they've taken her to the doctor."

His voice is getting a bit loud, but does that stop me?

"Well, I'd rather be at the doctor's than stuck inside that stupid box for an hour!"

That does it. He stands up and says, "It is obvious that you haven't spent enough time reflecting on why hitting someone is *never* a solution to a problem. Your mother has been informed that you will be suspended tomorrow, and when you come back to school, you are to shake hands with Heather and put this whole incident behind you. Is that clear?"

I stare at him. *"Suspended?"* I mean, I haven't even been in school a whole day. How can he suspend me? People get suspended for starting fires in the bathroom or for passing out cigarettes. But me? Suspended? For this? "You've got to be kidding!"

That makes him even madder. "This is no joke! And when you come back, I'd darned well better see an attitude adjustment, young lady!"

He practically pushed me out of his office, and then he made me sit in the front hallway for the rest of the day. When school was finally over, I didn't even bother to go back to homeroom for my backpack. I just ran home.

*   *   *

I'd gotten clear over to Maynard's Market when Marissa caught up with me. She swings off her bike and pants, "Sammy! Sammy, why didn't you wait?"

I shrugged. "I was too mad."

She walks next to me, pushing her bike, and I don't know why but she *whispers*, "Everyone's saying you got suspended!"

"Yeah."

"Cool!"

I stopped walking. "Cool? What do you mean, cool?"

"You don't have to go back to that zoo tomorrow. You get to do anything you want—that's cool!"

I rolled my eyes. "Right. I'll probably get grounded or shipped off to live with my mother. Real cool, Marissa. If you think being suspended's so cool, why didn't *you* punch Heather in the nose?"

"Aw c'mon, Sammy. She didn't stick *me* with a pin..." Then she says, "But I did go in and talk to Mr. Caan after school. I told him everything that happened."

"And...?"

She looked down. "And he says it doesn't matter who started it, you're not supposed to go around hitting people."

I just shook my head and punched the "Walk" button on the stoplight.

Marissa says, "Hey! Let me buy you a Double Dynamo."

Now normally I would've just said, "Nah, that's okay." I don't like Marissa buying me stuff, even though she tries to do it all the time. But I thought about it a minute and decided that, yeah, she could buy me an ice cream cone. It was hot, I was hungry, and it was on account of Marissa's not being able to tell Heather to bug off that I was in so much trouble—well, sort of anyway. So we turned around and walked into Maynard's Market.

And standing at the counter, with her mountain of hair looking extra shellacked, was the lady from the Heavenly Hotel.

SIX

I yanked on Marissa's sleeve. "*That's* who I've been trying to tell you about all day."

"Her? What about her?"

We duck behind a carousel of spicy pork rinds and I whisper, "She got robbed last night. Over at the Heavenly."

"Wow…"

"Yeah. And I saw the guy who did it through my binoculars."

Marissa's eyes bug out. "Cool!"

"Not exactly…He saw *me*, too."

"No! How did he see you?"

I give her a crinkly smile. "Would you believe I waved at him?"

Marissa's hands flew up to her mouth. "You *waved* at him? What were you *thinking?*"

"Apparently I wasn't."

We go back to watching the lady. She's wearing layers. I don't think you'd call it a dress, or a top and a skirt. It's just layers. Like she went to the fabric store, rolled around in a few bolts of flimsy fabric, then checked out.

Marissa whispers, "She looks like a Gypsy or something."

Now the lady's up at the front counter talking to T.J.,

41

only T.J.'s not really listening—he's looking for us. T.J. is Maynard's son. He works there about half the time, and Maynard's there the rest of the time. T.J.'s not as grumpy as Maynard, and usually he's too busy talking on the phone to pay much attention to you, but he likes having kids in the store about as much as Maynard does.

He calls out, "What are you two up to back there?"

I straighten up. "Oh, nothing. Just had to tie my shoe." I head over to the freezer and say, "We're just going to get a couple of drumsticks."

He leans to the side, watching us. "We're out of the Double Dynamos."

Well, then they're out of drumsticks as far as I'm concerned. And I know why they're out. T.J.'s why. He's always eating them. Grams will send me down for a quart of milk, and there he is at eight in the morning, chomping down a Double Dynamo. If you go there at night and it's all of thirty degrees outside, there's T.J., slurping up a Dynamo.

Marissa says, "Shoot!"

The lady notices me. "Hey! You're the girl from last night!" She turns to T.J. "If it wasn't for her, those cops wouldn't have done diddly-squat."

He nods like he couldn't be less interested.

"She saw the guy. Through binoculars."

He raises an eyebrow at me, then turns back to the lady. "So, are we on for tonight, or what?"

"Don't think I can, Teej. I've got a client coming at six."

"Aw c'mon, Gina. How long can that take?"

Gina gives him an annoyed look. "At least a couple hours. If you'd ever break down and let me do yours, you'd know that."

"You charge too much."

"I'd give you a deal."

He slides her a pack of cigarettes. "It'd still be too much. I can't believe people pay you for that mumbo-jumbo."

"It's not mumbo-jumbo. It's science."

T.J. rolls his eyes. "Science."

She passes him a ten-dollar bill. "Laugh all you want. It's not like I'm reading palms, and it sure beats working for my daddy."

He slams the register drawer. "Look, Madame Nashira, I'll be out of this hole before you. In a few years I'll be living out on Jasmine and you'll still be slumming at the Heavenly."

"In your dreams, honey."

Now when T.J. said, "Madame Nashira," Marissa's eyebrows popped way up and so did mine. See, there's a place on Main Street with zodiac signs all over it that says, MADAME NASHIRA, HOUSE OF ASTROLOGY. It's a few blocks down from the mall and Marissa and I have dared each other to go inside, but neither of us ever have. For one thing, it's got these dusty old drapes and you can't really tell what's inside, but also, it's kind of wedged between a bar and a pool hall. Grams would kill me if she ever found out I was even *walking* on that side of the street, never mind going into Madame Nashira's.

Marissa takes a step closer. "You're Madame Nashira?"

43

T.J. laughs. "Ooh, Gina—you got a fan!"

She scowls at him, then smiles at Marissa. "That's me, honey." She rips the cellophane off the cigarette pack and says to me, "What was your name again?"

"Samantha. Sammy. This is my best friend, Marissa."

Marissa says, "What do you do, tell fortunes?"

She snorts, "Only when I have to. I hate telling fortunes—it's so bogus. Guys'll come over from the pool hall or the Red Coach and want their fortunes told. What am I supposed to do? Tell 'em, Nah. I don't want your ten bucks? I gotta pay the rent." She lights her cigarette, blows smoke into the air, and says in T.J.'s direction, "So when I got a serious customer who wants their birth chart done, I'm not gonna just blow 'em off."

T.J. rolls his eyes again and lights a cigarette of his own. Gina says, "Hey, I thought Papa Bear didn't like it when you smoked in his store."

"Get out of here, would you?"

Gina laughs, "I'm gone," and flows out the door, trailing smoke.

T.J. shakes his head, then glares at us. "You two gonna buy something, or what?"

Marissa whispers, "Let's go try and find Oscar, okay?"

I nod, so T.J. says, "Well then get out of here. Scram!" He picks up the phone. "I've had enough female chat for a while."

*   *   *

Oscar's usually not too hard to find. He follows the same path every day; it's sort of a figure eight around the mall and up through the neighborhoods near St. Mary's Church. Once you get to know Oscar you've got to like him. He's just amazing, the way he pushes that cart of his around and sells ice cream to people. See, Oscar's blind.

Now not only is Oscar blind, he's also pretty deaf. So buying ice cream from him can be kind of complicated. You've got to shout out what you want, and then you can't give him anything bigger than a one dollar bill. When it comes to coins, though, you can give him any combination. He wears one of those coin dispensers around his waist and he's really good at pushing levers and making change. *Chinga-chinga-chinga*. He's fast, and he always gets it right.

Anyhow, when we stepped out of Maynard's we spotted Oscar almost right away, pushing his little cart along Broadway near the mall. We ran across the street, and when we were close enough to hear his bell jingling, we slowed way down so as not to startle him.

When we're close enough, Marissa calls out, "Hiya, Oscar! We'd like two Double Dynamos."

He stops his cart and then straightens out this old blue fishing hat that he wears to keep his head from burning. He pushes his dark glasses farther up his nose, cups his ear, and says, "A Double Dynamo, did you say?"

Marissa calls, "Two, Oscar. Two. It's Marissa and Sammy."

He smiles and moves his head a bit like he's sunning his face. "Well, good afternoon, ladies. Two Double Dynamos coming up."

He flips open the freezer and gropes around a bit, and

45

when he comes up with two Double Dynamos, my mouth starts to water. Marissa pays him, and *chinga-chinga-chinga*, he gives her some change.

He says, "Nothing like a Double Dynamo. Enjoy 'em, ladies," and starts jingling his way down the sidewalk.

Now a Double Dynamo is not just an extra-big drumstick. It's basically two scoops of ice cream double-dunked in dark chocolate and then rolled in peanuts until every last bit of it's coated. It's so big that they put a plastic protector around the top of it and wrap the cone in a nice fat napkin because there's no way you can eat the thing without making a mess.

So we sit down on the nearest patch of grass and get busy inhaling our ice cream. And just as I'm getting down to the cone, Marissa jumps up and says, "Is that *Mikey?*"

I look across the street and sure enough, there's Mikey coming out of Maynard's with a bunch of candy bars in his hands. I laugh. "Is there any doubt?"

"I don't believe it! Mom let him stay home from his first day of school because he was sick! C'mon!" Marissa starts racing back to Maynard's calling, "Hey! Hey, Mikey!"

Well, Mikey's picking up his bike, trying real hard not to drop any of his candy bars, when he hears Marissa yelling at him. He starts prancing around like he doesn't know which way to run, then jumps on his bike and takes off. Trouble is, he's so busy looking over his shoulder at us running toward him that he crashes into a newspaper stand and falls into the street.

By the time he's got everything picked up, Marissa's

grabbing him by the collar and yelling, "I can't believe it! You ditched your first day of school!" She shakes him. "Boy, are you gonna get it when Mom finds out you were clear out here buying junk food."

"It's not junk food!"

Marissa rips the candy out of his hands. "A Hershey bar, three Reese's cups, a Snickers . . . Mikey, *this* is junk food!"

"Well, I wanted a Double Dynamo but they were all out." He gives her a hopeful look. "They're not junk food. There's milk in those."

Marissa shakes her head and throws the candy bars— *thunk*—into a trash can. "Get on your bike—we're going home."

To tell you the truth, between finding out Gina was Madame Nashira and eating a Double Dynamo, I'd actually forgotten about getting suspended. But when Marissa calls over her shoulder, "Don't worry about school. Everything'll work out," it all comes flooding back.

And all of a sudden I'm real worried about Grams. I mean, I'm already late, and she's probably been waiting for me all afternoon.

So I start running. And in no time I'm pounding up the fire escape stairs, telling myself that Grams'll understand why I punched Heather in the nose if she'll just give me a chance to explain, when I get to the fifth-floor door and open it.

And there, sitting in a folding chair with her arms crossed, waiting, is Mrs. Graybill.

SEVEN

"Ah-ha!" she says. "Ah-ha!" Then she springs up from her chair and grabs me by the arm.

Now most people would've thought this woman was crazy, sitting at the end of the hall in her bathrobe and slippers, waiting for someone to come through the fire escape door. But I knew by looking at her that she was dressed and ready for action. Mrs. Graybill had lipstick on, and lipstick is her idea of being dressed. She doesn't brush her hair—it's got a flat spot in back where she sleeps on it, and it sticks straight out everywhere else. She doesn't put on shoes or clothes. She just puts on lipstick. Usually pink. And she goes *way* outside the lines. Especially on the top lip. It almost looks like she's wearing a little pink mustache up there, it's that bad.

So there she is, fully dressed, grabbing my arm, croaking, "I knew it! I just knew it!"

I look at her and try smiling while my brain's racing around for a way out of *this* one. I say, "Knew what?" like I'm the most innocent person you'd ever want to meet.

"Don't play dumb with me, girl," she says, shaking my arm. "This has gone on long enough! This building is government-subsidized for senior citizens—not entire families! If your grandmother thinks she can get away with having you live here at the government's expense, she's got another think coming!"

"But ma'am," I say, "I was just taking some of my grams' trash out for her."

"Ha!" she says like a big old crow. "I've been sitting here for over an hour, waiting for you to come through that door. I knew you were getting up and down somehow, but it wasn't until I noticed *this* that I figured it out." She opens the door, pries out my bubble gum, and shakes it in my face.

My brain's racing and I'm smiling the best I can, but my stomach's upside down and my knees are feeling kind of wobbly, like I'll be sitting down any minute, whether I want to or not. "Look, Mrs. Graybill, I don't live here. Really! Why would I want to live here? I just try to help my grandmother out as much as I can. Mom likes me to check on her 'cause she's not doing that well."

"Oh, baloney! Oh, baloney and hogwash!"

"Really! And just now I was down throwing away some trash and..."

"Why didn't you just use the trash chute?"

That takes me a second. "It was kind of a big box—it didn't fit. I took it down the elevator and then came back up the stairs. It's quicker, y'know?" I smile real big. "Want to come down to the Dumpster and see?"

She sputters around a bit and then hauls me by the arm down to Grams' apartment and pounds on the door. Grams opens it, looking healthy as ever, and Mrs. Graybill says, "I know this girl is living with you, Rita! It's against the law, do you hear me? Against the law!"

Well, Grams takes *her* by the arm and drags her into the apartment. "Take a look, Daisy! Does it look like a child lives here?"

So Grams is yanking on Mrs. Graybill, and Mrs. Graybill is yanking on me, and we're all moving across the living room like some kind of giant centipede when Mrs. Graybill says, "Let go of me!"

I say, "Let go of *me!*" and we all kind of look at each other and then let go.

Grams takes a deep breath. "Daisy, honestly, the girl just helps me out. It gets lonely here—you know that. Don't you wish some of your family would stop by every once in a while for a visit?"

"Every day is not once in a while!"

So Grams guides her around the apartment. First she opens the bathroom door; then she opens the bedroom door. "Do you see evidence of a child living here?"

Well, Mrs. Graybill's looking around, not saying much. Then we move into Grams' bedroom and Mrs. Graybill throws open the closet. And she's dying to say, "Ah-ha!" only none of my clothes are in there. She lets out a little sigh, and Grams says, "Daisy, can't you just give up the hunt? Wouldn't it be more fun to be friends?"

I'm thinking, Friends? With Mrs. Graybill? That's all I need! But lucky for me, Mrs. Graybill just pushes her lips out so she looks like a duck with a fat pink beak and storms out of the apartment.

Once she's gone, Grams' hands land on her hips. "So you've been suspended."

All of a sudden I'm so happy I could pop. I throw my

arms around her and say, "It *was* you! I was afraid that maybe…" Then I look at her and say, "What happened to the story about Aunt Valerie?"

"*Victoria*—and I completely forgot. And once I started pretending to be your mother, I couldn't exactly go back on it, now could I?"

I give her another hug. "Grams, you're the best!"

She blushes, then pushes me toward the couch. "Now, Samantha, you sit right here and tell me what happened. How in the world could you get yourself suspended on the first day of school?"

So I tell her. The whole thing. From the top. About Heather Acosta and her fire-engine hair and her earrings. About the way she made fun of my shoes and tried to mooch money from Marissa. About her sticking me with a pin and how I smacked her in the nose. Then I tell her about Mr. Caan putting me in the Box and how nobody but Marissa would even listen to me.

And when I'm all done I take a big breath because the whole story came out in one gigantic sentence, and what does Grams do? She puts her arm around me and says, "I wish I'd had a friend like you when I was growing up, Samantha Keyes."

Then she asks me what happened with Mrs. Graybill, so I tell her all about how she was waiting for me by the fire escape door and how she grabbed me by the arm and yelled at me and how I lied about the trash chute and the Dumpster and everything. Pretty soon Grams is looking worried.

"She found the gum," I say quietly.

Grams sighs. "It's only a matter of time, Samantha."

I look down. "What if I got a job? Maybe we could move?"

"That's out of the question."

So we sit there a while and finally she says, "You'll have to go out for a bit, so she thinks you've left."

I nod. "I know. It's okay." But what I'm thinking is how nice it would be just to stay home and watch TV and not worry about anything.

Finally I get up. "I don't feel like walking all the way over to Marissa's. Maybe I'll go over to the mall, or over to see Hudson."

"Oh, Samantha, no. Not over to Hudson's. You spend far too much time with him."

"But Grams, he's nice! You should come with me some-time."

She just shakes her head and says, "I just wish you had some more friends your own age."

I go into the kitchen. "I'd still visit Hudson." I rummage through a drawer until I find a roll of masking tape. I stuff it up under my shirt into my armpit and say, "Ready." Grams watches me, but since she doesn't ask, I don't explain. I just head for the door.

Once I'm outside I call, "'Bye, Grams! See you tomorrow!" so Mrs. Graybill will hear me leaving.

Grams calls back, "'Bye, honey! Thanks for the help!" and there I go, straight to the elevator, whistling away, putting on a show for Mrs. Graybill.

When the elevator shows up, I get on it and punch the fourth-floor button. Then, when the elevator stops, I get out and reach back inside and punch the lobby button just in case Mrs. Graybill's watching the elevator lights on our floor. After I check the hallway and the coast is clear, I hurry down to the fire escape and get to work.

Now a wad of masking tape doesn't work nearly as well as a nice fat piece of bubble gum, but after a while I got the jamb plugged and really, you couldn't even tell the tape was there if you weren't looking. I tested it a bunch of times, then took the elevator down to the lobby and made a lot of noise so that Mr. Garnucci would notice me leaving.

Normally I don't want Mr. Garnucci to notice me. He's the manager and practically lives in the lobby. He knows everybody, including me. He's not that old, but he talks like he's old—he tells the same story over and over again and talks really loud—probably from being around old people all day. So normally I try to slip right by him, but seeing how Mrs. Graybill probably called him and told him to be on the lookout for me, there I was, in the lobby, making a lot of noise.

Mr. Garnucci looks up from his paper. "Sammy! How's that grandmother of yours?"

I'm afraid to answer, because before you know it he'll be telling me about *his* grandmother who's ninety-four and still riding her bicycle. So I give him a quick wave and call, "Fine! See you later!" and duck out the front door.

I stand outside for a minute, thinking; then I cut across the parking lot and head straight for Hudson's.

Hudson has a one-story house with a big stone fireplace and a nice shady porch. He's also got more books than the library. His back room has shelves from the floor to the ceiling on all four sides, and every single one of them is crammed full of books. They don't look like they're in any kind of order to me, but if you ask Hudson a question he doesn't know the answer to, he'll mosey into his library and in no time he'll have a book that'll give him the answer.

When I got to Hudson's, I picked up his newspaper and headed right up his walkway. He wasn't on the porch like he usually is, but the minute I rang the doorbell the front door whooshed right open.

You'd know Hudson Graham anywhere. It's not his thick white hair and bushy eyebrows that give him away, though. It's his boots. If you ever see a man walking down the street in yellow or emerald-green or violet cowboy boots, chances are good it's Hudson Graham.

And there he was, in the doorway, wearing a pair of boots that looked like they should be combed instead of worn. I guess I was staring, because he grins and says, "They're wild boar—like 'em?"

Into my brain pops a picture of this giant mean-looking pig with enormous tusks and a snort like an air horn. I laugh. "It's going to take me a minute to get used to them." I hand him the paper. "Are you busy?"

"No, no! Stay a while. Can I look something up for you?"

"No thanks, I'm just here to visit."

"Great! Have a seat. I'll get us some refreshments."

So I sit in a chair on the porch, and I'm listening to the chimes from St. Mary's Church when a man turns up Hudson's walkway.

He's wearing a baseball cap and a windbreaker, and he's looking at the ground as he walks, so at first I didn't recognize him. Then I realize that it's the guy I bumped into at the mall.

It looks like he's going to come up to the porch, but instead he turns and follows the walkway around back.

I call out, "Hey!" but he just pulls on the bill of his cap and keeps right on walking.

And he's about to go through the back gate when Hudson comes out and says, "Evenin', Bill! Some mail arrived for you today. I put it on your bench."

The guy tugs on his cap again, then goes around the corner without a word.

"Who was *that*?"

Hudson hands me a glass of iced tea. "My new renter. Bill Eckert."

The back of Hudson's house is like a maze of converted rooms. He's got a workshop, a darkroom, a one-car garage for his car, Jester—they're all fun to snoop around in, and Hudson's happy to let me watch him when he's working on a project.

But then there's his regular garage, which he's turned into an apartment. Hudson won't let me anywhere near that without telling me not to bother his renter.

Hudson takes a sip of tea. "Bill's a bit of a loner, but that's okay." He flips open the paper and says, "You want the funnies?"

I'm still feeling a little strange about this guy being Hudson's renter, but I say, "Sure."

So I'm sitting there, sipping tea and reading the funnies, when all of a sudden Hudson's boots start tapping against each other.

55

"What's up?"

"Seven-twelve Cook Street, seven-twelve Cook Street." He puts down the paper. "I could hit it with a stone!"

"Hit what with a stone?"

"The house that got robbed last night."

"What?"

Hudson goes back to reading the article, "They're saying it's the sixth burglary in this vicinity in the past two and a half weeks."

I jump up. "Did they catch the guy?"

Hudson reads some more. "No."

"Well, did anybody get a good look at him, at least?"

Hudson dives back into the paper. "Hmmm...apparently not. It says here that the residents came home early from a dance recital because their daughter was taken ill. When they walked in, the burglar ducked out a back window..." He looks up at me. "I wonder..."

I'm staring at him, waiting, and finally I say, "You wonder what?"

He tugs on an eyebrow, then pops one of those furry boots up on the railing. "It sounds to me like they surprised him."

I think about this a minute. "Yeah...so?"

He gives me a little smile. "Sammy, you've got a decent set of marbles—you tell me. A family plans to go out for a couple of hours in the evening. Something happens and they have to come back early, and when they do, they find that some fella's in the middle of helping himself to their good silver..."

His eyebrows are pushed way up his forehead and he's

smiling at me like it's time for me to show off some of my marbles.

I say, "They came home early...they live close by..." just trying to buy myself some time. Then all of a sudden I can feel those marbles line up. "The burglar must've known they were going to be gone...He must know them!"

Hudson gives me a great big smile and swings his other foot onto the railing. "I'd bet my brand-new boots on it."

EIGHT

I let Hudson have the funnies while I read the article. When I finished, I handed it back and decided to tell him about what had happened at the Heavenly and how I was kind of worried about what I'd done. Trouble is, I didn't want him thinking I was a weirdo, looking in other people's windows and all. So I made the mistake of going on and on about how great binoculars are and what-all you can see with them from Grams' apartment window. And just as he's starting to look at me like, Okay, Samantha. Out with it, his dachshund, Rommel, comes hobbling onto the porch dragging something with him. At first I don't pay much attention to him—I'm getting ready to tell Hudson about waving at the hotel thief. But then I notice that Rommel's not dragging a branch or a bone. He's dragging a purse.

I slap my leg. "Come here, boy. What have you got there?"

Rommel comes scooting over, and that's when I notice he's all muddy. He lets go of the purse, then sits there smiling and panting, very proud of himself.

Hudson says, "Rommel! You've been digging again!"

Rommel keeps right on smiling.

The purse is in pretty good shape. And it's pretty full.

It's got makeup and gum and a hairbrush, a couple of pens and pencils, even a calculator.

Hudson's been looking over my shoulder, and when I get done rummaging through the purse he says, "Something's missing."

"The wallet."

He nods. "I wonder where Rommel found this."

There's a hard plastic photo-keeper attached to the zipper. I flip it back and forth. On one side is a girl about six or seven hugging a kitten, and on the other are two older boys, dressed in baseball uniforms. I show it to Hudson. "Do you know these kids?"

"Yes! These are the Keltner twins, and that's their sister, Elyssa. They live about four houses down." He turns to Rommel. "Where'd you find this, boy?"

Rommel smiles and pants, and you can tell—he wants his purse back.

Hudson gets up and marches his furry feet off the porch and around back. Rommel and I chase after him, and when we turn the corner what we see is trash all over the backyard.

"Rommel!"

Rommel looks at him like he's ready to chase a fox.

Hudson sighs, and we walk to the back fence where a trash can's been tipped over. Actually, it's more *dug* over. Rommel can't exactly jump, so he brought it down from underneath.

Hudson stands there a minute shaking his head. "Unbelievable."

"You can say that again!" I start picking up trash,

putting it back in the can. "Do you think the purse was in your trash can?"

Hudson peeks over the back fence. "Maybe somebody tossed it in from the alley?" He shakes his head. "Seems very strange."

"Maybe it didn't come out of the trash can."

Hudson looks around. "Then where did it come from?"

"Has Rommel been out? Maybe he brought it home."

"No, he can't get out unless he digs out, and I see no evidence of that."

So we picked up all the garbage and filled the hole back in, and then Hudson says, "Elyssa mentioned something about them visiting her aunt this week, so I have a hunch they're not home, but let's go down to the Keltners' and check anyway." He turns the purse over. "I wonder how long this has been missing."

We walk down to the Keltners' and sure enough, no one's home. Hudson picks up some newspapers cluttering up their yard and stashes them on their porch, then takes a last look around. "Let's go home and call the police."

So that's what we do, only I start worrying that Officer Borsch and Tall 'n' Skinny will be the ones to show up, so I say, "Hudson, I've really got to get back home. Grams is probably worrying about me."

On the way home I'm so busy thinking about the purse that I'm nearly up to the fifth floor of the fire escape before I remember that it's locked. I turn around and go back down to the fourth floor, let myself in, cruise over to the regular stairs and walk the rest of the way up.

And I'm waltzing down the hall when I turn the corner

and what do I see? Mrs. Graybill outside our apartment, talking to Grams.

I try to duck back around the corner, but I'm not quick enough. Mrs. Graybill sees me and says, "There she is! Rita, go get her!" Then she calls, "You come back here or I'll call the police!"

That stops me right in my tracks. I turn around and peek past the corner at them, and then I start walking toward them, wondering why in the world Grams is looking at me like she just bit into a lemon.

Mrs. Graybill shakes a napkin in my face. "What did you think? That I'd let you get away with this?"

"Get away with what? What is that?"

Grams looks down.

"This dumb-girl routine is getting very tiresome," Mrs. Graybill snaps.

"Daisy, let me handle this." Grams looks me in the eye. "Are you saying you didn't put the note under her door?"

I'm feeling like I'm in a basement without a flashlight. "*What* note?"

Mrs. Graybill shakes that napkin in my face again. "*This* note!"

When I finally got it away from her and read it, it felt like there was a centipede crawling down my back. I knew I hadn't written it, but I had a good idea who had.

I look at both of them and say, "I didn't write this!" but I can tell that Grams doesn't quite believe me.

Mrs. Graybill croaks, "Who else would write a note like this? Who *else*?"

I feel like telling her that it's the guy who's been stealing stuff from people all over town and that he's got the wrong apartment and thinks *she's* the one who saw him and waved. But what I say is, "I swear, Mrs. Graybill, I didn't write it. I would never write anything like this!"

"Ha!" she says. "It's just the sort of thing you would write!" She holds up the napkin. "'If you talk, you'll be sorry.' Is this supposed to scare me?"

Well, it was scaring the oatmeal out of me, but I just said, "I know why you think it's me, but it's not."

Mrs. Graybill turns to Grams. "Really, Rita, I've had enough. I think it's time I had this child banned from the building."

Grams takes a deep breath. "Go ahead, Daisy. If it makes you happy, go down and talk to Vince Garnucci about it. Samantha says she didn't do it, and that's good enough for me." She puts her hands on her hips. "Did you ever stop to think that maybe you've made some other 'friends' in this building? Maybe one of them left you the note."

"I don't even have any other friends here. I…"

"I wonder why!" Grams yanks me into our apartment and slams the door. Then, before I can thank her for sticking up for me, she snaps, "How could you?"

It felt like she just slapped me in the face. Then she says it again—"How could you? Did you really think it would shut her up? Don't you know it's as good as telling her she's right? What in the world do you expect me to do about this? First you get suspended for fistfighting, now you're writing threatening letters…Samantha, I'm beginning to feel like I don't even know you!"

I try to cut in and explain, but every time I do she starts scolding me some more. I feel like screaming, "Listen!" because I want her to believe me and I know I can make everything all right if she'd just listen to me.

So I'm saying, "Grams...Grams...*Grams!*" but when she finally turns to me and says, "What!" the phone rings.

And all of a sudden it's dead quiet in the apartment except for the phone ringing off the hook. Grams looks at me and I look at her, and finally she picks it up and says, "Hello?" real softly. After a second she pinches her eyes closed and I'm thinking that Mrs. Graybill has already told Mr. Garnucci everything and that this is him calling to say that Grams had better start packing. But what Grams says is, "No, she can't come to the phone."

That throws me, but I'm thinking, Okay, okay...at least it's not Mr. Garnucci. It must be Marissa.

Grams says, "I don't care if it *is* an emergency—she can't come to the phone."

So I'm sitting there, wondering what kind of trouble Mikey's gotten himself into this time, when Grams says, "The police? Why are the police looking for Samantha at *your* house?" She listens for another minute, then holds out the phone to me without a word.

NINE

It's Marissa, all right, and you can tell—she's dancing around with her cordless phone, biting on a fingernail, having a heart attack. "Sammy, you've got to come. Now! I told them you were in the shower. What is going *on*? They say you said you lived here! What am I supposed to *do*?"

"The *shower*?" My brain races around for a solution, but all I feel is marbles crashing into each other, going nowhere. "Are your parents home?"

"No."

"What about Mikey?"

"He's in his room, feeding his fish. I told him if he came out, I'd tell Mom and Dad about him going to Maynard's when he was supposed to be sick."

"Okay, okay. I'll be right there."

"How in the world are you going to get here?"

"I'm going to run."

"*Run?*"

"Yeah. Leave the back door unlocked and tell them I take long showers. I'll be there as fast as I can."

I hang up and look at Grams. She's sitting on the couch with her face buried in her hands, shaking her head. I run up to her and give her a hug. "Grams, I'm really sorry. I promise I'll explain everything when I get back."

She looks up at me and whispers, "Samantha, you act like you're running from the law."

I let out a nervous little laugh. "Actually, it's kind of the opposite. Everything'll be all right, I promise." I give her a quick kiss on the cheek, and as I'm leaving she says, "I'll be waiting."

I wave and close the door, and then I start running. Down the stairs, through the lobby, across the parking lot, and down Main Street.

Now, I walk to Marissa's house all the time. Before my skateboard got stolen I used to go to Marissa's house almost every day. But I'd never run to Marissa's house. And I guess I started off too fast, because two blocks down Main Street the iced tea I'd had at Hudson's locked up tight on my right side and wouldn't let go.

But I kept on running, holding on to my side like I'd been shot, feeling a hot spot on my little toe where a blister's going to pop up any minute, and by the time I turn up Jasmine I'm not running anymore, I'm hobbling.

I hobble up the hill as fast as I can, wondering the whole time if it's Officer Borsch who's waiting for me, and if it is, if he's figured out yet that I'm not really in the shower.

I cut through a neighbor's yard, then scrape myself up climbing over the fence into Marissa's backyard. By now I just want to lie down and die, but instead I drag myself up to the house, turn on a hose, then lean way over and drown my head in freezing cold water.

Marissa's head pops out the back door. "What are you *doing?*"

"Taking a shower! Quick—get me a towel!"

She comes back and throws me the towel. "Hurry! I think they're getting suspicious!"

"What do they look like? Is one of them really fat?"

"Yeah! And the other's really skinny. What is going *on?*"

"I can't explain right now. It's too complicated." I yank off my shoes and put the towel over my shoulders. "Let's go!"

We go charging through the kitchen and den, and then catch our breath right outside the living room. Marissa opens the door and says, "Here's Sammy," then smiles and backs way off into a corner to watch.

Now the McKenzes' living room is glass. Nothing but glass. Glass tables, glass shelves with little glass figurines, glass lamps, even glass *chairs*. And sitting there in one of those dainty glass chairs is Officer Borsch, looking like an elephant trying to squeeze into a fishbowl.

I smile at them and rub the towel on the side of my head. "Hi. Sorry you had to wait. What's up?"

All that leather gear and equipment around their stomachs kind of creaks and jingles as they stand up. "We'd like you to take a look at a few pictures, if you would."

"Sure."

I start rubbing the hair on the other side of my head, trying to act casual, but the whole time I'm wondering why in the world Marissa's pulling funny faces and jerking her arm back and forth like she is.

Officer Borsch pulls a photograph out of a big envelope. "Is this the fella you saw at the Heavenly the other night?"

Marissa's pulling faces like a blowfish and slapping at

air, and I'm doing my best to ignore her as he hands me the picture. Then I see Mikey, peeking around the living room door, looking like a bumblebee in a black-and-yellow shirt.

I check out the picture. "It's not him."

"Are you sure?"

"I'm sure."

"You didn't look at it more than a second, how can you be so sure?"

"I just am. I'm positive."

The Borsch-man wants to give me an argument, but Tall 'n' Skinny says, "Try the other one."

Officer Borsch pulls out another picture. "Take your time."

So I'm watching Marissa out of one eye, and I'm watching Mikey out of the other, and then Mikey decides—he's coming in.

I hand the photograph back to Officer Borsch. "It's not him."

Mikey pipes up with, "Let me see!"

Officer Borsch looks at Mikey, then back at me. "Who's this?"

I smile and say, so Mikey can't hear me, "My brother." I look over at Marissa like Help! because I know that any minute Mikey's going to give me away and then who *knows* what Officer Borsch will decide to do with me?

So what's Tall 'n' Skinny do? He turns to Mikey and says, "It's all right, son. We're just asking your sister a few questions about someone she saw."

Mikey grins at me like boy, has he got something over

on me or what, and he's about to spout off when Marissa comes flying across the room and yanks him back into the hallway. "Maybe we'll just wait outside . . ."

Mikey starts screaming and kicking, but Tall 'n' Skinny and Officer Borsch just kind of look at each other and shrug.

I try to distract them by asking, "So, has any more . . . uh . . . evidence turned up?"

Officer Borsch squints at me like he knows I'm up to something, but Tall 'n' Skinny says, "We've just had a purse turn up. It was reported missing almost a week ago and we think it's somehow connected to the other burglaries on that end of town. So if you remember any details about the man you saw at the Heavenly, please let us know." He turns to Officer Borsch. "I think we're done here."

Officer Borsch frowns and nods, and they start down the hall. And I guess with all their leather gear creaking and their equipment jingling they can't hear Mikey, sounding like he's under ten feet of water, screaming, "Let me out! Let me out!" I cough and excuse myself and cough some more, trying to cover up Mikey's voice, and the minute they're outside I race over to Marissa.

Marissa's got Mikey locked up in a closet and she's leaning on it with all her might. She sees me and says, "Oh, thank God!"

I pop the closet door open and look at Mikey like I'm going to kill him. He tries to charge past me but I grab him by the shirt. "Listen up, Mikey! If you tell *anyone* about this, Marissa's going to tell your mom and dad how you ditched school today and how you've been spending all your allowance on candy bars. If you keep your mouth shut, then so will we. Think about it, Mike. If your parents find out where you were today and what you've been doing with your allowance, you know what they'll do? They'll ground you for a *month*, that's what they'll do, and they'll take away your allowance. You got it? That means no more Fancy Fudge, no more candy bars, and no more Double Dynamos. They won't let you have anything but broccoli and fish. You hear what I'm saying? Broccoli and fish!"

He looks to Marissa for help, but she jumps right in. "I hope you do tell! Do you really think Mom and Dad are going to care that Sammy said she lived here? I don't even know why I'm making this deal with you. You're the one that's in hot water, ditching school like you did."

"Okay, okay! I won't tell!"

Marissa says, "Swear?" like she's a little surprised.

Mikey says, "Swear," and you can tell—for once he really means it.

Now what I should've done was start walking back home right then and there. What I did instead was walk straight to the refrigerator when Marissa offered me some orange juice. Grams was the furthest thing from my mind.

And then, of course, I had to explain everything. I told Marissa about Officer Borsch grilling me at the Heavenly, and when she found out I'd actually been *inside* the hotel she said, "Cool!" and wanted to know all about it.

So I told her about the pope-hat chairs and the guy with the cigar, and pretty soon we're talking about Gina and her crazy hairdo. And of course crazy hair makes us think about Heather Acosta, and all of a sudden Marissa says, "Say...maybe Gina is Heather's mother!"

Well, that makes me bust up so much I can't help it—I spray orange juice everywhere.

Now if I'd made it to the part about Mrs. Graybill and the note under her door, I'd've thought about Grams. And I'd've jumped right up and called her. Trouble is, we got so sidetracked making jokes about Heather being Madame Nashira's daughter that I completely forgot Grams was home worrying.

And when the phone rang, I still wasn't thinking about her—I was busting up at Marissa talking in a Texas accent, saying that if Gina was Heather's mom, then maybe they're both "hair from outer space."

Marissa answers the phone and she's laughing so hard she can barely say hello. And when she finds out it's Grams, she keeps right on laughing and just hands over the phone.

Well, of course I'm not thinking about anything but alien hairdos, so when I take the phone and put it up to my ear, I'm still laughing. Until I hear Grams' voice. Then all of a sudden I don't feel like laughing at all.

She says, "I take it the emergency's over."

"Grams—I'm sorry! I was going to—"

"Don't bother. I don't want to hear it. You realize I've been worried sick about you?"

Now I try to tell her I'm sorry and I try to tell her I'll be right home to explain everything, but she keeps cutting me off. Finally she says, "Let me talk to Marissa."

"But—"

"*Let me talk to Marissa!*"

Now you have to understand—Grams had never shouted at me before. Never. Not when I left the water running in the sink and it overflowed, not when I burned the potatoes so badly we had to throw the pan away, not when I spilled grape juice on her new couch, or broke her favorite teacup. Grams just doesn't yell. At least that's what I'd always thought.

But there she was, yelling at me. And all of a sudden I've got this enormous lump in my throat and there's no way I can talk. I just hand Marissa the phone.

Marissa says, "Uh-huh . . . They'll be home pretty soon . . . Uh-huh . . . That'd be fine . . . Uh-huh . . . Okay, sure . . . 'Bye."

I grab her arm. "What? What did she say?"

Marissa smiles. "You get to spend the night!"

Grams isn't wild about me spending the night at Marissa's since her parents go out so much, and with me being suspended and all, well, it just seemed kind of strange. "How'd *that* happen?"

"Don't worry about it—this is great!"

Then it hits me. Grams doesn't want to see me. She's so mad at me she doesn't want to see me. So I ask Marissa if that's why I'm spending the night. She bites a fingernail and tells me no, of course not, but what she's really saying is yes.

I try to call Grams back, only she won't answer the phone. I know she's there, watching it ring off the hook, but she won't answer it. And as I'm standing there listening to it ring I'm feeling like the last one picked for teams—like being stuck with me is worse than being one short.

Pretty soon the lump in my throat is making it so I can't breathe, let alone think. I hang up, and before Marissa can stop me I lock myself in the bathroom.

And sitting there in the middle of the bathroom floor, surrounded by turquoise tile and turquoise towels, I bury my face in my hands and cry.

TEN

Marissa's parents finally showed up around eight o'clock. They put down their briefcases, gave me big smiles, and said, "Why, hello, Samantha, how are you?"

I lied and told them I was just fine, and wondered if Mrs. McKenze would be mad if she knew I'd used their shower, eaten two of their Lean Cuisines, and was wearing her daughter's clothes.

Mr. McKenze went straight to the phone, to call in about stocks somewhere, I suppose. They're always on the phone, especially Mr. McKenze. Either on the phone or at the computer. Mrs. McKenze says it's the only way to stay "on top of the game." Marissa says they even take a phone to bed and set alarms during the night so they can get up and check on overseas stocks, if you can believe that.

Mrs. McKenze pours herself some bottled water and says, "Marissa, dear, your father and I are planning to go up to Big Falls this weekend. Can you think of anything you might need while we're gone?"

"Can I come?"

Mrs. McKenze flutters around a little. "Well, dear, you know how much your father and I need a break—I was hoping I could count on you to look after Michael?"

Marissa looks down. "Oh."

"How *is* Michael anyway?"

"Well enough to go to school tomorrow."

Mrs. McKenze smiles and says, "Excellent! Maybe I should go check on him . . ." Then off she goes to check on the little faker.

Marissa whispers, "Let's go up to my room, okay?" and you can tell—something's bothering her.

Marissa's room is more like a fancy hotel suite than a bedroom. She's got two beds, a window seat full of teddy bears, and her very own bathroom. Marissa's bathroom is always a mess. The sink has toothpaste in it, the floor's covered with dirty clothes, and there's not a glass figurine in sight. It's the best room in the house.

The minute we close the door, Marissa flops down on the bed, hugs a pillow, and sighs. I flop down on the other bed and say, "What's the matter?"

All of a sudden Marissa's crying. "Why can't we go with them? We never get to go anywhere together! It's not like they're actually going to relax up at the lake—they've got two phone lines and a computer up there! And it's not like I'd be in the way or anything."

So I say, "Maybe they—" but before I can get it out, Marissa lets out this scream. I jump up. "What? What?"

She points to the ceiling, all bug-eyed, and whispers, "What is that?"

I look at the ceiling and what do I see? Nothing. "What's what?"

She points again. "That!"

I stand on her bed and take a close look at where she's pointing, and sure enough, there it is: the teeny-tiniest spider on earth. I look at Marissa and laugh. "How did you even *see* it?"

Well, she's not laughing. Not one bit. "Is it a spider?" All of a sudden it drops and she screams and holds her face just like in an old black-and-white movie.

I reach up and slap the spider between my hands and when I open them up, there's barely even a smudge on my palm.

I go rinse my hands off while Marissa tries to recover from the heart attack she gave herself. When I get back she says, "They are so creepy!"

"It was microscopic!"

She shivers. "Little spiders grow into big spiders." She plops back down on the bed and sighs, and a second later she's forgotten all about the spider. "All I really want is for them to be home once in a while. I'm so tired of frozen dinners and Pop-Tarts. They always tell me I've got to be home for dinner, and then they don't show up until eight o'clock or something. I can't believe how lucky you are."

I shake a finger in my ear like I need my hearing checked. I mean, here she is in her very own bedroom with her very own bathroom on one of her two beds in a gigantic house she shares with both parents, calling *me* lucky. Marissa's never had to worry about which way to sneak into the house or how to pay for some little thing she decides she wants at the mall. Never.

So I say, "Lucky? Me?"

"Yeah, you. Your grandmother's *always* home. Any time you want to see her, there she is, waiting for you. If I want to get ahold of my mother, I have to go through about twenty 'Please hold's before I can talk to her, and then she's usually in the middle of some deal and winds up telling me she'll see me when she gets home. Thanks a lot, Mom."

"But Marissa, you do get to see them every day. And they're really nice to you—they give you anything you want!"

Marissa makes a face. "Yeah. 'Here's some money, kid, now leave me alone'—I just hate it!"

"The money?"

"Yes, the money! The stupid money." She looks straight at me. "You're the only friend I've got. The only one. You're the only one who's never asked me for money. You won't even take it when I try to give it to you!" She whacks a pillow with both hands. "Every time I think someone's being nice to me 'cause they like *me,* what do they do? They ask to borrow money. It's always the money."

Well, I think about this a minute. I mean, even though Marissa has everything in the whole wide world, I've never actually wanted to *be* her.

We were quiet for a long time, just lying there on our beds. And I'm in the middle of wishing I could be at the Senior Highrise sneaking past Mrs. Graybill so I could give Grams a hug and sleep on her couch, when Marissa does something I've never heard her do before: she snores.

I watch her for a while, lying there flat on her back with her mouth wide open, snoring. Then for some reason I think about a spider dropping from the ceiling right into her mouth, and I bust up.

Marissa doesn't wake up, though. She just keeps right on snoring. So I chuckle about the spider some more and then get up to turn off the lights.

And when I go back to bed I stare out the window at the moon, wishing for morning so I can get home and explain everything to Grams.

ELEVEN

In the morning, Marissa offered me a ride on her handle-bars, but I figured out a long time ago that Marissa McKenze is not someone you should accept a ride from. The one time I did she about killed me, wobbling all over the place, telling me to duck so she could see where she was going, putting on the brakes so fast that I fell off and almost cracked my skull. No, it's much safer to walk, even with the world's biggest blister telling you to ride.

So off she went, racing down East Jasmine, waving and wobbling, calling over her shoulder, "Wish I'd been suspended!" and off I went, wishing I'd drained my blister.

When I finally got home, I let myself in, and what I'm expecting to see is Grams on the couch reading the paper or doing a crossword puzzle or watching the morning news. But what do I see? Nobody. I call out, "Grams, I'm home!" and what do I hear? Nothing. So I peek into her bedroom and say, "Grams...?" and then check the bath-room. "Grams?" Finally it dawns on me: Grams is not home.

Now this had never happened before, and it struck me how *quiet* it was. And then I started to worry. I moved around the apartment from place to place, not really going anywhere. First I sat on one side of the couch; then I sat on the other. Then I moved across to a chair and just sat there with Dorito in my lap, staring off into space. I wondered where in the world Grams could be. I mean, what if something had happened to her? Maybe she was in the hospital. Maybe Mrs. Graybill had come after her with a curtain rod or something. Maybe...maybe she hadn't answered the phone when I'd called last night because she was in trouble.

Then I had a terrible thought: maybe the hotel thief had come back looking for me and wound up tying Grams up and stuffing her in the closet.

Now I tell myself that's stupid; it couldn't have happened. But the more I think about it, the more I can just see her, tied up with duct tape, her glasses all crooked, shoved in the back of the closet.

So I get up. And very slowly I move to Grams' closet. And I'm standing in front of it, feeling like I've got X-ray vision because I can just see her in there, and I take a deep breath, yank open the door, and...there's nobody there.

Well, I feel pretty stupid, and before you know it I'm back in Grams' favorite chair, worrying. And when I'd had just about as much worrying as I could take, I got up and started vacuuming. I vacuumed the whole apartment. Even the baseboards. All that noise helped me think. And what I decided was that if Grams was home in the morning, then she was probably all right. If she hadn't been home all night, then there really was something to worry about.

I shut off the vacuum cleaner and headed for the kitchen. I checked out the sink, which was empty; then I looked inside the dishwasher. The bowl on the top rack had been rinsed, but when I looked at it real closely I could see some oatmeal stuck to one side. I checked the glasses and there was a spot of pink on the side of one of them. Grams' grapefruit juice.

So I closed the dishwasher and went into the bathroom. Sure enough, Grams' toothbrush was wet. So was the bottom of the bar of soap. Well, I felt a lot better. Grams was fine, no doubt about it. And I was just about to leave the bathroom when I noticed something in the wastepaper basket. I bent down and picked it up, and sure enough, it was what I thought it was—tissue paper with lipstick dabbed on it.

Now I've only seen Grams wear lipstick for real special occasions, so it was strange, finding the shape of her lips on that piece of tissue paper. And I couldn't help thinking I missed something. I mean, what was the special occasion? Where had she gone?

So I started sweeping up the kitchen, scrubbing down the sink, cleaning out Dorito's litter box, just keeping busy while I was trying to figure it out. But after all that cleaning I still didn't have an answer, so I sat down and had a big glass of milk and waited. And waited. And waited some more. And pretty soon I'm sick to death of waiting and I'm thinking about what in the world I can go do. Going to the mall doesn't sound like any fun. The Pup Parlor would be all right, but I don't really feel like it. Then I remember how I really should get some gum to replace the masking tape on the fourth floor, so I head to Maynard's.

Nobody's in the market but T.J. And since he's on the phone with his back turned, I decide to check out the comic books. And I'm back by the magazines when I hear him say, "What do you mean the crop froze? How can the crop freeze? It's always ninety degrees in Florida!" He listens for a second, then says, "Hugh! Buddy! You told me it was a sure thing! 'Double your money overnight,' that's what you said. . . . I know there are risks, I know you can't guarantee . . . but you said it was a sure thing! No no no, *you* don't understand. I borrowed it from my old man. I've got to make it back by the end of the week or I'm out of a job, out of a home, out of . . . " He listens for a long time, then shakes his head. "Man, you said that last week about coffee beans. You said that Friday about oranges! Now you're talking pork bellies? Give me a break." He listens for a long time. Finally he sighs. "You better turn this thing around, Hugh. . . . Yeah, go ahead. I'm in for the pork bellies."

He gets off the phone, mumbling, "Pork bellies . . . " and then he notices me. "Hey, you're not supposed to read those here! You're supposed to buy 'em and read 'em at home." He goes to the freezer and takes out a Double Dynamo. "What are you doing here anyway? I thought school started yesterday."

I check out the freezer, which is chock-full of Double Dynamos, then count the money in my pocket. Not enough. I look at T.J. chomping away on his and say, "I got suspended."

His eyebrows shoot up. "Suspended? On the first day of school?"

I pick out some gum and pop it on the counter. "That's right."

He stares at me and I just stare back. Finally he rings me up and says, "Get out of here, would you? I don't need juvenile delinquents hanging around my store."

So I stand on the corner of Broadway and Main awhile, watching cars do-si-do around each other, and all of a sudden I get a very bad idea. And the more I think about it the more I talk myself into believing it's a good idea, and off I go down Main Street, straight to Madame Nashira's House of Astrology.

I wasn't really expecting her to be there. I tried peeking around the old velvet curtains, but I couldn't see much, so finally I pushed on the door. A bell jingled as it opened, and a voice called, "Not open, sorry!"

I stood there blinking for a minute, trying to get used to the darkness. The walls and the ceiling were painted black, with little silver stars everywhere. There was an old velvet love seat, and in front of it was a coffee table with unlit candles and a big deck of cards. Across the room was an ancient-looking telescope on a brass stand, and sitting at a table next to it, punching numbers into a calculator, was Gina.

The table had a thick green skirt around it, and behind it was a white curtain, coming down from the ceiling like a slice of the Milky Way.

I watched her for a minute as she went back and forth between a book and the calculator. Finally I said, "Hi."

Well, she about jumps into outer space. And when she comes back down she's clutching her heart. "Don't *do* that to me! I was concentrating!"

"Sorry..."

She looks at me a little closer. "Oh, it's you!"

"Hi."

"What are you doing out so late?" She gropes for her watch and curses.

"What's the matter?"

"That creep took my watch, too. Like he's gonna be able to get anything for it. It's just silver plate, but I really liked it. It had moons on one side of the band and suns on the other and...Doesn't matter. It's gone." She eyes me. "The point is, what are you doing out so late? Does your mama know where you are?"

I laugh. "It's ten in the morning!"

"No kidding?"

I pull back the window curtain. "See?"

She shields her eyes like I'm torturing her. "Put it down!"

I drop the curtain and laugh. "Sorry!"

"So why *are* you here?"

"Um...I don't know...I guess I was hoping that maybe they'd found out something more about..."

"The jerk who stole my money? No chance. Not with that buffoon in charge." She squints at me. "Why are you so interested, anyway?"

I just shrug and stand there in front of her desk, toeing the carpet with my high-top.

She studies me a minute. "You're not just interested— you're worried!"

I keep digging at the carpet. "No I'm..."

"Yes you are! What's the matter? You worried that maybe the guy saw you, too?"

I look up at her. "I know he did."

"Seriously?" She gives me a doubtful look. "How do you know that?"

I go back to destroying the carpet and mumble, "Because I waved at him."

Her face twitches a minute, and then she busts up. "Oh, you're priceless!"

"More like stupid."

She laughs a little more, then makes herself stop. "Look, honey, you're probably worried about nothing. Maybe he saw you, but he can't know who you are. It's too far away."

"I keep trying to tell myself that, but..."

"So what you've got to do is get your mind off of it. Forget about him. Make yourself think about something else." She taps the paper on her desk. "Ever had your birth chart done?"

"I don't even know what a birth chart is."

"You don't? Well, sit down and let me show you!"

She's looking at me so excited, I can't exactly say, No thanks, I really shouldn't even *be* here, so down I sit, right across the table from her.

She shoves this drawing at me that looks like a cross between a clock and a wagon wheel. "*This* is a birth chart. It plots out the exact position of the planets at the time of someone's birth." She points to the wedges. "These are houses. That's the way we divide up the space surrounding Earth. There are twelve houses, and each one represents a sphere of human life.

"For instance, the first one is the house of Aries and

Mars. It reveals personality and psychological motivation, whereas, say, the sixth house—Virgo and Mercury—is related to health, diet, and exercise."

Now when Gina started talking about the birth chart it's like she became a different person. She still looked like a Gypsy who'd dunked her head in a bucket of shellac, but all of a sudden she sounded different. She sounded really smart.

She sees me staring. "Why're you looking at me like that?"

I blink. "Sorry."

"Okay. Like I was saying, these are the houses and this"—she points to a green line going through the middle of the chart—"is the horizon."

"The horizon?"

"Yeah. The horizon at the time of birth. You need to know that so you can position the cusp of the first house. That's called the ascendant."

"The ascen-what? What's a cusp?"

She laughs. "Here. This line is a cusp. It separates one astrological sign from another. The ascendant is the degree of the zodiac rising over the eastern horizon at the moment of birth. Each degree takes about four minutes to rise."

"Wait a minute. How do you know the moment of birth?"

"You need a birth certificate. Gotta have it. You can't just guess 'cause even if you're only a few minutes off, by the time you're done making all the conversions into sidereal time your whole chart'll be off. Same with the place of birth. If the latitude and longitude are off, well, forget it."

"Seems pretty complicated to me." I look at her chart for a minute. "So what do you *do* with it?"

"I'm not anywhere near done yet! I've got to finish writing in the glyphs, draw in the midheaven, position the sun and the moon and the planets. Then I've got to draw in the aspects, progress it, and interpret it."

I shake my head. "Wow."

She studies me a minute. "You're an Aries."

It's not a question, but I nod anyway.

She laughs. "Who but an Aries would wave at a man stealing money?" She collects her papers and says, "What I want to know is, what else have you seen through those binoculars? You some kind of Peeping Tomasina?"

I can feel my cheeks turning red. "No! I just...well, sometimes I get bored."

Gina nods like she understands. "Ever try looking at the stars through binoculars? It's pretty cool."

"Really? They're so far away I wouldn't think you could see them any better."

She slides her papers into a drawer and straightens out the books. "Try it sometime. You'll be surprised." She points to the telescope across the room. "Last year around Christmas I hauled that thing to the roof of the mall. It was spectacular!"

My mouth drops open. "The roof of the mall? How do you get up there?"

"Haven't you ever gone behind one of those 'Employees Only' doors?"

"No . . ."

"They'll take you straight to the roof." Gina laughs. "And here I thought you were an anarchist." She picks up her keys and says, "Bedtime for Madame Nashira."

I watch her lock up and go, and the minute there's a break in traffic I jaywalk across the street so I don't have to walk through the guys already hanging around the Red Coach. And before I even reach the far side of the street I've got a whole new plan for how I'm going to spend my day.

TWELVE

Mrs. Graybill's nose wasn't in the hallway, and Grams' binoculars *were* under the bed—right where I'd left them. I cleaned the lenses, scrawled Grams a note, then headed for the mall.

When I got there, I tried to act real casual riding up the escalator, but since the only people at the mall in the middle of a school day are adults and babies, it felt like everyone was staring at me. Like any minute someone was going to come right out and say, "What are *you* doing here? And, hey...what's with those binoculars?"

The second I got to the top floor I found an "Employees Only" door and ducked behind it. I stood there for a minute, just glad to be away from all those adults and babies and eyes staring at me. Then I started walking.

I'd always thought there were just bathrooms behind those "Employees Only" doors. I didn't know there was a whole maze of corridors! And I'm cruising along, feeling like a hamster in a new cage, when a door swings open and practically knocks me over. It's not an adult, and it's sure not a baby—it's Brandon.

He flips back that shiny hair of his and says, "Sammy! Sorry."

I said, "What are *you* doing here?" because everyone knows Brandon's supposed to be at school.

"I had a dentist appointment. I just stopped by to pick up my paycheck." He looks me up and down. "I might ask you the same question..."

I blush and mumble, "I got suspended."

"Suspended—*you?*"

I check out my high-tops, feeling pretty stupid. "Yeah. For punching someone in the nose."

He laughs. "Well, I'm sure they deserved it." Can you believe that? I tell you, Brandon's all right. Anyhow, he looks at his watch and says, "I've got to run. I'll talk to you later."

I stop him. "Hey, Brandon? Do you know how to get up to the roof?"

"The roof? Why do you want to get on the roof?"

"I don't know, I just do."

He pulls on the back of his hair, studying me a minute. Finally he says, "Go down this way and turn left at the next T. It's the first door on the right." He turns to go, then stops and says, "You didn't hear that from me, right?"

I laugh. "Right!"

I ran down the corridor and turned left, then opened the first door on the right. It led to some cement steps, and up to another door.

I went up the steps and through the door, and all of a sudden there I was, on the roof of the mall. And it felt like I was on top of the world. I ran around a bit, peeking over the edge of the roof wall; then I cut through a bunch of fans that looked like the top of some Saudi sheik's palace and went over to the other side. I could see the tops of trees and power lines and the roofs of houses. And then people—lots of people—just kind of hurrying along the sidewalk.

After I'd looked around with my eyes, I started using the binoculars. First I checked out the Salvation Army. There are always people hanging around at the Salvation Army. They kind of spend the day sharing cigarettes and lying back on their sleeping bags, watching people go back and forth to the courthouse, waiting for someone to come out of the soup kitchen with some food.

I spent a little while watching them watching people, and then I decided to watch the people they were watching. Lawyers mostly. They were hanging around outside the courthouse, sharing cigarettes and talking, looking quite a lot like the people at the Salvation Army, only dressed up. It didn't take long to get tired of watching them, so I moved on over to the police station.

The police station is right next to the fire station, so you'd think there'd be a lot going on, but there wasn't. I watched the front door of the police station for a long time and it only opened once. Same at the fire station. I could see a couple of guys cleaning the fire trucks, but it all seemed like it was in slow motion.

So I cruised along the wall for a while, watching some bulldozers level dirt for a new mall parking lot, and then I thought to look for William Rose Junior High School. Maybe I could even spot Heather Acosta picking her nose or something.

I found the school all right, but all I could really see were the basketball hoops, so I gave up and went over to the other side of the roof. There were people sitting on benches in the little grassy area around the mall—mostly in the shade, because it was pretty hot out. There was a lady with her baby, sitting under a tree playing peek-aboo. There were a couple of guys drinking out of Styrofoam cups, playing checkers. There was a man in a three-piece suit, and with his briefcase and perfect hair I would've been sure he was a lawyer, except he was doing something you never catch lawyers doing: he was eating an ice cream cone. A Double Dynamo.

Well, I looked down the street a little farther and sure enough, there's Oscar, sitting on a planter by himself in the shade of a big tree, cleaning his glasses with a hanky, enjoying a rest from pushing that cart of his around. And all of a sudden I realize that the roof of the mall is the hottest place in town and I'm dying for an ice cream—or at least a drink of water.

So I start for the door, telling myself I'll come back when it isn't so hot—maybe at night, to check out the stars—when I get the idea to look for Hudson's house.

So I run across to the far side of the roof, then find Hudson's house with just my eyeballs. I put the binoculars up, adjust the focus, and sure enough there's Hudson, sitting on the porch, beating the heat with a tall glass of iced tea, laughing.

And sitting right next to him, beating the heat with a tall glass of iced tea, laughing, is my grandmother.

* * *

I felt like going down to Hudson's but I didn't. I went home. And the longer I waited for Grams, the madder I got. What was she doing? Trying to teach me a lesson? What if I hadn't seen her through the binoculars? And why was she spending the whole day with someone she thought *I* spent too much time with?

When she finally came through the door, she was hauling a bunch of plastic shopping bags, humming. She put them down on the kitchen counter and smiled at me. "Did you have a nice day?"

I crossed my arms. "I was *suspended*, remember?"

She starts taking cans out of a bag and putting them away. "Oh, I remember all right."

I watched her for a minute. "This was just your idea of teaching me a lesson, wasn't it?"

She keeps humming away, putting up the groceries. Finally she turns to me and says, "I'm sorry, Samantha. Really. I didn't mean to be gone so long."

Huh. I'm quiet for a while, then I heave a sigh. "Worrying's the pits."

Grams throws her head back and laughs. "You can say that again!"

And she's on her way over to give me a hug when I say, real quietly, "At least when you worry about me it's because of emergencies—not because I decide to spend the day sipping tea on someone's porch."

That stops her cold. "What?"

"Have a nice time with Hudson today?"

She takes her glasses off and starts buffing them, holding them up to the light, then buffing them some more. "I only went there because I thought it was high time I knew a little bit more about the man."

"Because of me?"

"Yes, of course, because of you."

"So...? I'm right, huh?"

"I'll agree he's a very knowledgeable man, but frankly I find him to be an insufferable flirt."

"An insufferable flirt? *Hudson?*"

She pops her glasses back on her nose. "That's right. But if you think for one minute you can make me forget your recent behavior by talking about Mr. Graham, you are sorely mistaken." She points to the couch. "Sit. Right now. Sit and talk. You've got a lot of explaining to do."

So I sit. And I talk. And I tell her right off that I didn't leave Mrs. Graybill that note—that I think somebody who knows I saw him steal something left it. Then I back up and tell her about the burglary at the Heavenly Hotel, and when it comes out that the binoculars were involved in the trouble I'm in, Grams is just dying to say, I told you so! but she doesn't. She just sits there, real quiet, looking paler and paler. And when she finally can't stand it anymore, she says, "Why in heaven's name did you *wave?*"

I shrug. "Grams, I don't know—I just did, okay?"

She looks at me through her glasses like Mikey looks at some new fish in an aquarium. "And next I suppose you're going to tell me you didn't call the police because you didn't want to worry me?"

My face crinkles up—part smile, part cringe. Then I add really fast, "But I *have* talked to the police. There's this guy named Officer Borsch—I told him the whole story that night at the Heavenly Hotel and—"

"At the Heavenly Hotel? You mean to tell me you went *inside?*"

My face crinkles up again. "Well, there were police cars parked out front, and I wanted to find out what was going on, so I—"

"You are *never* to set foot in that hotel again! Do you hear me? Never!"

"But Grams...it's not seedy, it's really kind of neat. It's got—"

"I don't care what it's got! It is no place for a girl your age, do you hear me?"

Just then the doorbell rings. Grams puts a finger to her lips and I do a quick check for anything of mine lying around; then I duck into the closet. Two seconds later Grams calls, "Who is it?"

Normally I shut Grams' bedroom door when I dive into the closet, but this time I didn't. I just dived in, made myself some room in the middle of Grams' shoes, and got ready to wait for whoever rang the bell to go away.

Then I heard something I couldn't believe.

I opened the closet door just a crack and sure enough, it was the voice of Officer Borsch. He was saying, "Yes, ma'am, I'm aware of that, but your neighbor insists that she's the one who left the note and it's my duty to follow up. It *is* a threat, you know."

Grams says, "Of course it's a threat! And if you'd catch that fella my granddaughter saw across the way, you'd have the person who left the note!"

"Ah, so *you're* the grandmother." It's dead quiet for a minute, then he says, "And I suppose it's your granddaughter who told you the note under your neighbor's door was left by the hotel thief?"

"That's right, and—"

He snorts. "With all due respect, ma'am, maybe this is just her way of getting some attention?"

By now I've pushed the closet door open a little more so I can hear better. And I'm dying to jump out and tell Officer Borsch a thing or two, but I can't. I have to just sit there, getting madder and madder, listening to him make fun of me. Then all of a sudden his voice starts to get louder and I can hear him creaking and jingling my way. He says, "Would you mind if I took a look out the window? I'd like to see if it's even possible to see the hotel room from here."

Now I can tell that the last thing in the world Grams wants is for Officer Borsch to go nosing through her apartment, but what can she do? He's already nosing.

His feet walk right past the closet, so I scrunch back as far as I can and hold my breath. I hear him mumble, "Mm-hm..." like he just doesn't believe it. Finally he says, "Where is your granddaughter, ma'am?"

"Home from school, I suppose."

"Ah, yes. She does have a very nice home, doesn't she?"

I can tell Grams doesn't quite know what to say to *that*. "Uh...yes, yes she does."

"So why does she come here so much? Your neighbor seems to think *this* is her home."

Uh-oh is what I'm thinking. Uh-*oh*. And I just know that Grams is out there sweating, but what she says is, "Oh, Daisy. She's...lonesome, if you know what I mean?"

Officer Borsch is quiet for a minute. Finally he says, "What's the name of the street your granddaughter lives on again?"

Well, my heart's going full speed ahead. I can see the Big Lie just crumbling away in front of me. Then, very quietly, out of Grams' mouth comes "East Jasmine."

Let me tell you, I felt like whooping. There's nobody in this world like my grandmother. Nobody.

And I'm sitting there, with my hands in fists, going, Yes! Yes! Yes! as loud as my brain can shout, when something brushes against my shoulder. Not Grams' coat. Not one of her dresses.

Something alive.

THIRTEEN

I had company. And I'm not talking a clothes moth or something. I'm talking *big* company. All of a sudden my heart's exploding and I can't breathe, and what I want to do is jump right into Officer Borsch's arms and cry, Help!

I turn my head just a little bit and crank my eyes over as far as they'll go, and there, staring at me from behind Grams' winter coat, are two of the biggest eyes I'd ever seen. I tried screaming but nothing came out. Nothing.

Then in a flash, he jumped out from behind all those hemlines, knocked over a stack of shoe boxes, clawed across my back, and high-tailed it out the door. My little buddy, Dorito.

And he left the closet door wide open.

Now it's one thing that he scared me to death. It's another that he made all that racket. But in the middle of all those adult shoes, sticking out like raisins in a chocolate-chip cookie, are a pair of high-tops. A pair of high-tops with legs coming out of them.

Officer Borsch jumps a few feet off the ground himself. He creaks and squeaks and says, "What the—?"

The next thing you know, Grams is going on and on about her mischievous cat, and the closet door is swinging closed. And I'm in the dark in the middle of an avalanche of shoes, safe again.

97

Now sitting there in the dark waiting for Grams to come back and tell me the coast is clear, I started thinking. First about Officer Borsch and how he didn't believe me. And he didn't, I could tell. Something about the way he looked at me when I was over at Marissa's—something about the way he said, Mm-hm...when he was looking out Grams' window at the Heavenly Hotel. Officer Borsch thought I was a liar.

Then I thought about Mr. Caan not believing me about Heather Acosta, and how even Grams had almost believed Mrs. Graybill over me. Why did everyone think I was a liar? Being trapped in the closet was starting to feel like being stuck in the Box, and suddenly all I wanted was to bust out from under all those shoes and hemlines and *prove* that I wasn't lying.

And tickling the back of my brain was this feathery kind of feeling that everything I needed was in there, just kind of spinning around in my skull, looking for a way to line up. And when it did line up I'd know—I'd know why the guy at the Heavenly Hotel looked so familiar, and why it was taking me so long to remember.

*   *   *

Marissa called me that night. She told me how all anyone at school wanted to talk about was how I'd broken Heather Acosta's nose.

"I *broke* it?"

"Yeah, she's got it all bandaged up, and brother, is she milking it for all it's worth. She's saying how you should've gotten expelled instead of suspended."

98

Now what I really felt like doing was laughing. Not because I'd broken Heather's nose, but because I could just see her running around with her torch top and earrings and a taped-up nose.

"She told me to tell you she hopes you learned a lesson. Can you believe that?"

"She hopes *I* learned a lesson?"

"Yeah, and this girl Tenille went around all day trying to get people to donate to the Help Heal Heather Fund."

"The *what*? Who's Tenille?"

"Some copycat friend of Heather's. I saw her in the bathroom before school, clamping on a bunch of earrings. Someone told me she'd do anything for Heather 'cause she thinks she's the coolest."

"And what's this fund for? They gonna buy her crutches for her nose or something?"

Well, that got Marissa laughing, and hearing her laugh made me laugh, and pretty soon we're just busting up, talking about two little crutches hanging out of Heather Acosta's nose.

Then, when we're both catching our breath, Marissa says, "She asked me for money."

"Heather did?"

"No, Tenille. She said it was partly my fault that Heather's nose was broken, so I should contribute to the fund."

I almost didn't ask because I was afraid of what I might hear, but I couldn't resist. "Well, did you?"

"No! I told her to drop dead. I told her you were my best friend and anyone who pricked you in the butt with a pin deserved to have her nose broken."

I tossed that around some and decided that what Marissa probably said was "Sorry, I don't have any money today." So I said, "Thanks, Marissa, but what did you really say?"

"What do you mean? That *is* what I said. Exactly!"

Well, I couldn't help smiling. I mean, Marissa McKenze finally told someone to bug off and she did it sticking up for me.

Then Marissa says, "So what did you do today? Did you have fun on your day off?"

Grams was taking a bath, but I still kept my voice down when I told Marissa about going into Madame Nashira's House of Astrology.

"No way! Without me? That's no fair!"

"So next time *you* punch Heather in the nose!" Then I told her about running into Brandon and snooping around on the roof of the mall, and how I'd discovered Grams at Hudson's, and about how Mrs. Graybill called the police. And I'm in the middle of telling her how Officer Borsch mm-hmed while he looked across at the Heavenly Hotel, when she pipes up with "We should go there!"

"What do you mean? Go where?"

"To the Heavenly—we should *go* there!"

Well, I know exactly what Grams would say if she knew we were talking about going over to the Heavenly Hotel—it would be a very short conversation starting with the letter N and ending with the letter O.

I stretched the phone cord as far as I could get from the bathroom. "No way!"

"Why not? You said it was cool!"

"Yeah, but—"

"Come on. Just for a minute? We'll just go in, check it out, and leave."

I twisted the cord some and huddled up to the wall. "Now?"

"Sure! I could be there in ten minutes."

"How about after dinner?"

"Cool! Meet me in front of Maynard's at what, seven?"

"Okay."

I got off the phone feeling like I'd just made a big mistake. I wandered into Grams' room and peeked through the curtain at the big pink "Heavenly Hotel" sign coming on across the street. And I started thinking: of all the rooms at the hotel, why did the guy pick Gina's? Did he know there was money in it?

And standing there, staring at that pink sign buzzing in the air, it hit me—Marissa and I were going into the Heavenly Hotel, all right. Only it wouldn't be for just a minute.

*   *   *

Marissa's never on time. Unless she's waiting to see the inside of the Heavenly Hotel, I guess, because there she was at seven sharp, waiting for me in front of Maynard's.

I said, "Hey! You ready?"

She starts biting a nail. "Are we really going to do this?"

"Sure. C'mon! This was your idea, remember."

When we get to the Heavenly Hotel I say, "Now listen. This is no big deal. Just act like you belong."

She whispers, "What do you mean, like I belong?"

"You know, like it's your house."

"Oh, okay," she whispers.

So I whisper back, "Do you talk like this in your own house?"

She blinks. "No..."

"So stop whispering!"

I open the door and march right in, and there's the same guy, chomping on a cigar, keeping an eye on the other people in the lobby from over the top of his newspaper. There are two men in the pope-hat chairs. One is wearing a corduroy coat and old Nikes and is sitting near the window reading the last few pages of a tattered paperback. The other is wearing a jogging suit and has his feet up on a coffee table. He's leaning way back, blowing smoke rings toward the ceiling.

But the cigar chomper isn't watching the two of them as much as he's keeping his eye on two *other* men huddled up near the staircase. They're both dressed in blue jeans and T-shirts, one of them's carrying a small paper bag, and even though they're keeping their voices down, you can tell they're having some kind of an argument.

A man with blond hair and a goatee comes out of the elevator, and as he's passing by the front desk the cigar chomper nods at him. The blond guy stops and says, "Ed says to send up his mail if any's come. I'll be back in a day or two to check on him, maybe bring him some smokes."

So while Cigar Man is busy listening to him, I give Marissa a nod and head for the stairs.

She grabs me by the arm and whispers, "Where are we going?"

"Up. C'mon."

Her ears move back a little like someone's pulling her by the hair. "Really?"

I just smile like I know what I'm doing, but my heart's starting to skip around inside because it knows I don't. "Sure. Come on."

When we're about five steps away from the staircase the blond guy takes off and Cigar Man growls at us, "Going somewhere?"

I look at him and say, "Mmm," in a way that could mean yes or no—who knows? I sure didn't.

He folds his paper and kind of pushes his lips out with that cigar right smack-dab in the middle. He shows his teeth and says, "What was that?"

All of a sudden Marissa walks right up to him like a wind-up toy that's about to pop a spring. "This is such a cool hotel! It's awesome!" She notices the funny green tiles on the counter. "Sammy! Come here. Have you seen these?"

Well, the guys by the stairs quit arguing, the man by the window puts down his book, and those smoke rings seem to just hang there in the air. I move over to the counter and keep my voice down as I say to the guy, "We were just going to visit someone we know."

He throws his head back and laughs. And that cigar's bobbing up and down, about to fall out, when all at once he stops laughing, puts down the paper, and growls, "Don't mess with me. You're not here to visit anyone." He rolls the cigar to the other side of his mouth. "You've had your little look-see. Now skedaddle!"

Marissa makes a beeline for the door, but I grab her by the shirt and kind of bungee her back. "Actually, sir, we *are* here to see someone."

He raises an eyebrow and Marissa looks at me like, "We are?" He gives me a hard look, then says, "Hey...you're the gal that was here the night of the ruckus."

I smile at him. "Yes, sir. And I was on my way up to see Gina."

"Gina, hmm?"

I shrug. "Or Madame Nashira...whatever you want to call her."

He chomps on his cigar for a minute, staring me in the eye. Finally he picks up the phone. "Let me see if she's in."

She's in all right. He tries to keep his voice low so we can't hear, but we can anyway. "Gina? Yeah, there's a couple of kids here to see you—the girl that was here the night you got hit, and some friend of hers...You sure?...All right, I'll send 'em up." He puts the phone down. "She's in four twenty-three. Fourth floor, turn right. Knock twice."

I say, "Thanks," and off we go.

Now from the lobby, the Heavenly's stairs look like just an ordinary staircase. But after the first four steps you turn left and all of a sudden you're in the middle of all these *mirrors*. No kidding. There's a wall of mirrors on both sides and they're a little bit warped, so you're surrounded by a lot of mutant reflections of yourself. And all those reflections kind of go on and on forever, because one wall's bouncing them off the other.

Anyhow, we make it up to the fourth floor, head down to 423, and knock. Twice.

Gina answers the door, looking like she just got up. She wraps the tie of her bathrobe and says, "Come in, come in," with a cigarette wagging up and down in her mouth.

By now I've gotten the idea of what Grams meant by "seedy." The wallpaper's peeling off, the paint's pretty dirty, and looking across the room I can see the bed's lopsided and the mirror on the far wall's cracked in two places.

Marissa and I are standing there staring at each other, each wishing the other one would just say, "C'mon, let's *go*," when Gina says, "Well, are ya comin' in or what?"

So in we go.

She says, "Sit!" and points her nose at the bed.

So we sit, kind of on the edge of the bed, and watch as she tries to rake her fingernails through her hair. And I'm wondering, How do you start over in the morning with a hairdo like that? It's all kind of clumped together and sideways and strands of it are sticking straight out in places looking like something a plumber would find in your pipes and say, "Aha! Here's your problem, ma'am."

Marissa nudges me and flicks what's left of her fingernails with her thumb. "Wow."

I don't know if she's thinking, Wow, has she got a lot of chewing to do! or Wow, that's some paint job on those nails, because Gina's fingernails aren't black with moons and stars anymore. They're silver with black comets shooting across them.

Gina takes a long drag off her cigarette, then rakes the hand with the cigarette through her hair.

Now I'm starting to worry about fire. I mean, she's whipping that cigarette around right next to about a gallon of hair spray, and I can just see them coming together to light up her head like the Fourth of July.

She rakes a little more while she's looking at us gawking at her, and finally she says, "So. Here you are. Wanna tell me why?"

"Well, actually, I was wondering—do you think whoever stole your money knew it was there?"

She blows some smoke straight up and it kind of gets lost in her hair for a minute before floating away. "I don't know how he could've."

"Well, was anybody else's room broken into?"

She shakes her head. "Just lucky little me."

I look over at the door. "Is that a new doorknob?"

She smiles out of one side of her mouth. "That it is. The creep snapped the other one right off."

"He snapped it off?"

She taps some ashes into a Styrofoam cup. "With a vise grip or pliers or something. At least that's what the cop said."

"Officer Borsch? He was up here?"

"We're talking about the fat one, right?"

I nod.

"Yeah, he was up here. For all of thirty seconds."

I stand up and look out the window, watching the cars go by for a minute. Then I check out the Senior Highrise and decide it's easy to get mixed up on which apartment's ours and which one's Mrs. Graybill's.

Finally Gina says, "Whatcha lookin' for?"

I look down to the intersection. "Nobody knew about the money? Nobody?"

"Nobody." She's shaking her head but all of a sudden she freezes. "Wait a minute—" Then she shakes her head again. "Nah."

"What? What were you thinking just now?"

She rakes her hair again. "Never mind. It's nothing." I stare at her and she says, "I ran into a girlfriend of mine, all right? Down by the corner store. I didn't even know she was in town. We got to talking, that's all."

"Well, what were you talking *about?*"

She looks at me like it's none of my business, but then says, "The usual. Appointments. The weather. You know."

"And you said something about having a bunch of money?"

"Not exactly. I mean, I might've said something about going to open a bank account in the morning"—she takes a deep breath—"'cause I didn't like carrying so much cash around." She adds real fast, "But Candi wouldn't do a thing like that to me—we're in the same kind of boat, if you know what I mean."

"Well, how about her boyfriend or something? Maybe she told him about it."

"She doesn't have a boyfriend." Gina shakes her head. "I shouldn't even've brought it up. There's no connection. Zero."

I think about this a minute. "You said you didn't know she was in town—did you give each other your addresses?"

Gina blows smoke through her hair. "Sure. I told her I was

staying here—big deal. It wasn't her, so drop it, all right?"

"How about somebody that overheard you talking? Was there anybody else around?"

She looks out the window and mutters, "We were standing right there, having a smoke . . ." She turns back to me. "How do I know? I don't think so. There wasn't anybody standing next to us, if that's what you mean. Maybe some people came in and out of the store, I don't know. I just don't remember."

"What about T.J.? How long have you known him?"

She snorts. "That loser? For years. He'll never change."

I say, real quietly, "Did he know about the money?"

She shrugs. "I don't think so." Then she laughs and says, "He hasn't got enough initiative to pull something like this off. Teej is much too lazy."

"Even if he was having money problems?"

She hesitates. "What do you mean?"

"I don't know exactly. He was talking to some guy on the phone about coffee beans and pork bellies—something about borrowing money from his dad."

She frowns a bit and says, "T.J.? Borrowing from Maynard? That's bad news." She looks down the street. "You think Teej did it?"

"I don't know! I don't even know where you were when it happened. How come your purse was home and you weren't?"

She shivers and grinds out what's left of her cigarette. "I *was* home. I was in the shower. I didn't even know someone had been here until I noticed the doorknob was busted. Nice piece of work, huh?"

My brain's starting to tingle a little. "Is the guy with the cigar down there all the time?"

"André? Yeah, he is. I swear he sleeps there."

"So how's a guy come into your room and steal your money without André seeing him first?"

Her jaw drops a little. "That's a good question. That's a very good question!"

We all look at each other a minute; then Marissa breaks the silence. "Maybe the guy who broke in lives in the hotel."

Gina rakes her hair. "Oh, *that's* a happy thought."

After a minute she starts up another cigarette so I say, "Well, we'd better get going. Maybe you should call the police and talk to them about all this."

She blows out smoke. "Yeah, maybe I should! I mean, why didn't *they* ask me any of this?" She walks us to the door. "I appreciate the concern, honey. Thanks for coming."

We wave and say 'bye, and Gina's about to shut the door when she pops back out and calls, "Hey! Don't go that way! Those stairs'll make you puke. Take the elevator." She waves her cigarette. "It's at the end of the hall."

Marissa and I look at each other and shrug, then head over to the elevator. And we're standing there waiting for it to open up when Marissa says, "This place gives me the creeps."

I nod and say, "No kidding," and that's when I notice something. There's a door at the end of the hall that's got a push bar instead of a knob, and even though there's no sign telling me so, I know it's not a janitor's closet.

The elevator dings and clanks open and I say, "Hold on a sec, okay?" and then hurry over to the door.

I'm about to push on the bar, but something stops me. Instead, I push on the door without touching the bar and sure enough, somebody's jammed the latch to keep it from catching.

"Marissa, come here! Quick!" I look outside, down four flights of fire escape stairs.

Marissa comes running over. "What's going on?"

I check the jamb, sure I'm going to find something wadded up inside it, but there's nothing there. Then I notice something on the ground. Crammed along the bottom edge of the door, keeping it from closing all the way, is this paper napkin rolled up so tight it looks like a piece of dirty chalk. I pick it up and unroll it.

And scribbled across the napkin are the letters HH. And underneath them, the number 423.

FOURTEEN

"Holy smokes!" Marissa says when I show her the napkin.

All of a sudden I want out of there. I say, "C'mon!" and before you know it we're pounding down the back side of the Heavenly Hotel like our underwear's on fire.

We wind up in the middle of a bunch of gnarly bushes and garbage, fenced in by chain-link on one side with really high cinder-block walls on either end. And I know there must be a way out, but it feels like we're trapped.

I climb up the chain-link a ways and say, "C'mon! There's a vacant lot on the other side."

Normally chain-link's pretty easy to climb, but this fence wasn't tied down to the posts, so it was really wobbly. And the higher we got, the more it leaned back until it felt like we were going to pull the whole fence down.

So we're almost to the top, swaying back and forth with the fence clanking like the chains of a ghost, when Marissa loses her footing and falls.

"Hey, are you all right?" I call.

"I—I think so," she says, but you can tell—she's landed pretty hard.

I call, "Hang on," and come clanking back down.

Marissa swears she's okay, so I start digging around the trash, looking for something to tie the fence back to the post. Mostly there's just paper and candy wrappers and bottles and cans, but finally I turn over this beat-up lettuce crate and underneath it is an old tennis shoe. I take the shoelace out of it and rub it along a link of the fence until it snaps in two. Then I reach as high as I can and tie the chain-link to the post. After that, I climb up, wrap the other piece close to the top of the fence, and flip myself over the top. "C'mon! It's easy now!"

Marissa does great until she gets to the top. I'm on the ground, waiting for her to swing her second leg over, when I hear, "Oh, no....Oh, no!"

"What's the matter?"

She's all twisted up on the top of the post. "I'm *stuck*."

"Just hold on to the post and swing your other leg over. You'll be fine!"

"But I can't—I'm stuck! My pants are caught!"

"Just unhook them!"

She says, "I can't!" and she sounds pretty scared.

So up I go to unhook her pants, and I'm halfway up when the top shoelace snaps and the whole fence starts bending back. Marissa screams and her pants rip and there she is, with one leg on each side of the fence, her underwear flashing like a flag of surrender.

I yell, "Hold on to the post! Hold on to the post!" because it looks like she's about to fall.

She pulls herself to the post and hangs on, shaking. Finally she swings her leg over and starts coming down, one little step at a time.

I help her down and when she lands she's still real shaky and doesn't want to go anywhere right away. So we head across the lot to this old crooked pepper tree that has branches drooping all around like a giant hula skirt.

We duck underneath the branches so Marissa can have some privacy while she's checking out the rip in her pants, and after a few minutes she peeks back at the Heavenly and says, "That was *scary*."

I laugh. "It was your idea, remember?"

She laughs, too. "Bright idea!"

I take the napkin out of my pocket and study it some more; then I hand it over to Marissa and ask, "Do you recognize this?"

She takes it from me. "It's a Double Dynamo napkin!"

"It sure is." All of a sudden spiders are dancing on my back again. "You know, I think the note that got shoved under Mrs. Graybill's door was on a Double Dynamo napkin, too."

"Are you sure?"

"I only saw it for a second, but yeah, I think it was." I look at her. "You want to go to the police station with me?"

She shows me her pants. "Like this? No way!"

"Aw c'mon, Marissa. What's a little rip in the pants?"

"This is no little rip! It's bad enough we have to go clear up to Wesler Street to get back to Maynard's. There's no way I'm going to the police station."

"We could take a shortcut—I bet there's a way through at the back of the lot."

She scowls at me. "Yeah, like the last shortcut we took."

"No, really. Look. See these bike tracks? They go straight through here...." And I'm following these parallel bike

113

tracks to the far end of the tree, pushing aside the branches, about to show Marissa that the tracks lead to a short-cut, when they stop.

Marissa thinks that's real funny. "Aw...too bad. I really wanted to get stuck on top of another fence." She walks toward the sidewalk, laughing and holding up the seat of her pants.

I still can't quite believe the bike tracks don't go anywhere but after I think about it for a minute I decide that kids must just park their bikes under the tree when they come to hang out in the shade. I catch up to Marissa and pretty soon we're turning onto Broadway, hurrying toward Maynard's.

That's when I notice a police car parked outside the Heavenly. I look at Marissa and she looks at me and says, "No way, Sammy! I'm not going back in there! We just ripped up my pants getting *out* of there."

"Just for a minute? Don't you want to know what's going on?"

"No. There is no way!"

Turns out we didn't have to go in because while we're busy arguing, Officer Borsch comes out.

He does a double take when he sees me, and right away he gets in my face. "Where do you get off going in there like that? You rile people up and then I have to talk myself blue in the face trying to convince them there weren't any clues then, there aren't any clues now, and there are never gonna *be* any clues!"

Well, let me tell you, there's nothing *blue* about Officer Borsch's face. It's as red as a hothouse tomato. And looking at him, well, I try real hard to keep the corners of my mouth down, but it's hard. I mean, I can just see it—there's the Borsch-man, all saddled up with guns and flashlights and batons and stuff, having to take it while Gina blows smoke in his face and yells at him.

His forehead's getting redder and redder and sweat's starting to drip down his sideburns. "Listen, girl, you stay away from this hotel, and you stay away from police business. I don't have the time to deal with your shenanigans!"

I'm thinking about that napkin in my pocket, trying to decide whether I should show it to a guy who looks like he's about to pop his thermometer. Part of me's saying Forget it! but another part reminds me that somewhere, pretty close by, is a guy I waved at while he was taking money out of a purse.

So I reach into my pocket and pull out the napkin. "Actually, I was on my way over to the police station 'cause I thought you might want to see this."

For a minute he just stands there, steaming. Finally he says, "What is it," like he doesn't really want to know.

I hold it out a little farther. "It's something I found rolled up in the fire escape door of Gina's floor. It was keeping the door from latching."

"What were you doing nosing around..." he starts, but then he decides to shut up and take the napkin. He looks at me, then back at the napkin and mutters, "HH, four twenty-three." He squints at me. "Just how did you find this?"

So I tell him about taking the elevator and seeing the door and about how it wasn't latched, and when I'm all done he says, "Is that so."

I didn't really like the way he said it, so I said, "Yeah, that's so. And in case you hadn't noticed, it's a Double Dynamo napkin. My grandmother told me you came over about the note that her neighbor got. I only saw it for a second, but I think it's a Double Dynamo, too."

He's still looking at me like I'm some dumb kid, so I say, "I thought you might want to compare the handwriting...?"

He squints at me. "You're clever. You're *real* clever."

I squint back at him and say, "What?" because he's acting like he thinks I'm lying.

He gives me a smug little smile. "I know what you're trying to pull here."

I take a step back. "What are you *talking* about?"

"You think I can't see through all of this? You write a threatening note to an old woman and then, to throw the blame on a burglar you *claim* you saw, you manufacture a clue and pretend you found it over at the Heavenly Hotel." He forces out a laugh. "Of course the handwritings are going to match. They're both yours!"

Well, my jaw must've about touched my high-tops. I couldn't believe what I was hearing.

Marissa says, "Now wait a minute!"

He just smirks. "Clever. Very clever." Then his face scrunches up so his eyes look like vents in the crust of a pie. "I'll take this into evidence all right, and if you ever, *ever* try to mess with me again I'll see to it that you spend some time away from that ritzy little house of yours." He throws open the police car door. "Remember that the next time you decide to manufacture some evidence."

Marissa and I just stand there with our mouths wide open. Finally she whispers, "Unbelievable."

I nod. "Yeah. Next thing you know he's going to decide *I'm* the one who stole Gina's money." And even though it sounds ridiculous, part of my brain's telling me that if I don't figure out who did, that might be exactly what happens.

FIFTEEN

Grams knew right away that I'd been up to something. I gave her a hug when I walked in the door and she pulled back. "Where have you been?"

I didn't want to say the mall or Hudson's or something because that would've been a lie, so I just said, "Walking around with Marissa."

That wasn't a lie, but somehow Grams knew it wasn't the truth either. She put her hands up on her hips. "Walking around where?"

All of a sudden I'm wishing I *had* gone to Hudson's or to the arcade or to the pet store for that matter. At least I would've had something to say. But I hadn't, so I didn't. I just kind of snapped the loose rubber of one high-top with the toe of the other and said, "Well, if you really want to know...I had to talk to Officer Borsch."

Grams takes off her glasses and starts huffing and buffing. Very calmly she says, "About...?"

I snap the rubber some more. "Oh, you know. The note that was left under Mrs. Graybill's door, the guy at the Heavenly—stuff like that." I look up from my snapping and I can tell she's not buying it. "Really, Grams! That's what I did!"

She pops those glasses right back on her nose and kind of leans at me. "Young lady, one does not reek of cigarettes after having visited the police. One does not reek of cigarettes after having simply 'walked around.'" Her eyes drill through me like little lie-detector lasers. "One would, I imagine, reek of cigarettes after one visits the Heavenly Hotel, though." She stares at me a minute while I'm busy tearing up my shoe. "Unless you want to tell me you've taken up smoking?"

"No, Grams! Of course not!" Then I blurt out, "How can you still smell it? It's been at least an hour."

She gives me a little smile. "Since . . . ?"

I flop down on the couch and sigh. "Since I went to the Heavenly to ask Gina some questions."

Grams' eyebrows pop way above her owl glasses. "Gina?"

"You know—the lady who got all that money stolen? And really, Grams, I'm not going back. The place is seedy. You're right, all right? It's seedy."

"Well, well, well," she says, like I told you so. "And what made you change your mind?"

"The staircase, for one thing." So I tell her about the mirrors, and then I kind of get carried away and tell her about Gina's room and how she shouldn't be too surprised if one of these days she's looking out the window and sees a fireball in 423 across the way—that it'll just be Gina's head running around the room looking for a bucket of water.

Grams just sits there very quietly, listening, but when I get to the part about Officer Borsch yelling at me she jumps up and says, "Of all the *nerve*." She flips through the phone book, muttering, "I'm going to give that obnoxious toad a piece of my mind. . . ."

"Grams, no! It'll just make things worse—they'll send him over here to talk to you and I'll be stuck in the closet in the middle of all your shoes. . . . It doesn't matter, Grams, really! He won't believe you no matter what you say."

She thinks about this, then sighs. "I suppose you're right." We're quiet for a minute, then all of a sudden her eyes light up and she says, "Say! I know!" and off she goes to her room. A minute later she comes crinkling back, carrying plastic bags, saying, "When I was out earlier, I picked up a little surprise for you."

Now you have to understand, Grams doesn't surprise me with anything. There are things I would want—like a new skateboard or a Walkman or even a watch—but I would never ask for them, and I would never expect her to surprise me with one of them. So when she says "surprise," my ears perk up like Dorito's do when I shake around his box of kibble.

"Really?"

She sits right next to me on the couch. "Just wait until you see this."

Well, believe me, I'm doing my best to peek in and do just that. She reaches into one of the bags and what does she pull out? Wool. Wool and a pair of knitting needles. She says, "Now, I don't expect you to jump up and down for joy—I just expect you to give it a chance."

It's good that she wasn't expecting it, because I sure wasn't doing any jumping. "But Grams . . ."

She just shoots me down with her eyes, and before you know it she's whipping that wool around, her fingers flying in between those clicking needles like mice teasing a crocodile. She says, "This is called casting on," and in no time she's straightening out a row of stitches, looking very pleased with herself. "Come here," she says, so I scoot a quarter of an inch closer. "Come *here*," she says again, so I scoot over.

She shows me how to knit and she shows me how to purl and before you know it I'm holding those needles, knitting and purling about as fast as a swimmer in mud. After a while Grams says, "See there? You're doing fine."

I just roll my eyes at her.

"You wait and see. In a few rows you won't want to stop."

She opens the other bag and pulls out an embroidery project. You know, the kind that's all sealed up in thick plastic with a picture on the front of what you wind up with when you're all done. Those pictures aren't really accurate, though, because they never show any blood spots on them.

Anyhow, I probably would've just stuck to my swimming in mud and ignored the picture of Grams' project altogether if she hadn't flipped it over so fast. Real fast. Like she didn't want me to see it.

I stopped swimming. "What's that?"

"Oh, just a project I thought I'd start on to keep you company." She pulls out the instructions and pushes the picture aside.

"Let me see, Grams."

She waits a second, then says, "It's just something I decided to make for St. Mary's bazaar this year."

"Well what is it?"

She flips it over and says, "Striking, isn't it?"

I'm expecting flowers poking out of a vase like she made last year, but what do I see? A fence post with a pair of cowboy boots resting on it. And since it doesn't seem like the kind of thing Grams would like, I ask her, "Are you feeling all right?"

She laughs. "I'm just tired of doing the same old thing." She goes back to reading the instructions, and after a minute I go back to tangling wool. And when we've both worked for a little while, she sighs and says, "I sure wish we had some of those pecan shortbreads in the house, don't you?"

Now you can *have* pecan shortbreads. They taste like the crumbs from the bottom of a toaster, all scrunched together. But Grams wanting some was all the excuse I needed. I tossed down my needles and said, "So do I. I'll go down to Maynard's and get some."

Grams looks at me. "Really?" Then she shakes her head and says, "No, no. It's getting too late . . ." but you can tell—she's got her heart set on toaster-crumb cookies.

I check the clock. "Maynard's'll still be open. Really, Grams, I don't mind."

"But—"

"And Mrs. Graybill's probably in for the night so you don't have to worry about her. I'll be right back!"

"Okay! We'll have cookies and tea and work on our projects. It'll be fun!"

*　　*　　*

T.J. was holding the phone with one hand and ringing up a customer with the other, so he was too busy to notice when I walked in. And when I found the shortbreads I kind of hung out in an aisle and listened while the other customer left. T.J. says into the phone, "No, man. I got it covered. As long as I've got it by tomorrow....That's cool with me....I'll get it to you by the end of next week at the latest....Yeah, man. Later."

He lights a cigarette, so I go up and put the cookies on the counter. "Your dad coming back soon?"

He blows smoke in my face. "What's it to you?"

"Just wondering."

"Well, go wonder someplace else, would ya?" he says, and gives me my change.

"Just looking forward to seeing a friendly face in here." I smile because everyone knows—Maynard's the grumpiest guy on earth.

"Funny. Very funny. Now scram!"

I take the shortbreads and I'm heading home when I decide that it wouldn't hurt to run over to Hudson's and ask him a quick question.

So I take a little detour down Cypress Street and there he is on the porch, watching the world go by. I wave and run up his walkway. "Hi, Hudson! Got a minute?"

"Sure, Sammy. What a nice surprise! I was just going to cut into a chocolate cake I baked this afternoon. Care for some?"

"I can't. I've really only got a minute."

Hudson eyes my cookies. "On an errand?"

I nod. "I'm supposed to be learning how to knit right now."

He laughs. "Knit? You?" He cuts me a piece of cake anyway. "So what's the burning question?"

"I've got two of them. First off, what are pork bellies?"

"You considering investing in pork bellies?"

"Hudson! I don't even know what they are. Look, T.J. was on the phone the other night talking about pork bellies—"

He shoves over the slice of cake. "Maynard's T.J.?"

"Yeah. He was talking about pork bellies and coffee beans and oranges. He seemed pretty upset—like he'd lost a bunch of money."

Hudson shakes his head. "Poor Maynard. That boy is going nowhere fast."

"So what are pork bellies?"

Hudson cuts himself a piece of cake. "Sounds to me like the man is playing the commodities market. Maybe futures, maybe options. Whichever, it's a surefire way to lose a bunch of cash in a hurry."

"What do you mean?"

"I consider it to be a sucker's game. Options brokers will tell you that you can double your money overnight— and sure, sometimes it happens, but by and large you lose money. With futures you can lose big money—more than you put in."

I take a big bite of cake. "I don't get it."

"Okay. Let's say your broker calls you up and tells you that the price of, say, silver has never been so low, and that you could make a quick buck by investing in silver options. He tells you that in all of human history, you could never get silver for less, and he's sure that because of some happenings in, let's say, Japan, the price of silver will go through the roof by the end of the week. He tells you that if you invest five thousand dollars at the present price of silver, when the price skyrockets later that week, you'll be set for life. Then, later that week when the price of silver *drops*, he comes back to you and says you've got to invest some more—it's never been this low, it's *impossible* that it'll go any lower. So you wire him some more money and pretty soon you've lost your shirt."

"That sounds like gambling."

Hudson nods. "Just like gambling. Some people win; most people lose."

"Wow."

"So T.J.'s up to his ears?"

"I think so. And I think it's Maynard's money."

Hudson shakes his head. "Maynard should've given him the boot years ago. The boy's a leech."

So I'm sitting there eating chocolate cake, thinking, and my brain's getting all tangled up. Why had the hotel thief looked familiar? Was he wearing a disguise? Was it T.J. under all that hair? I tried to put T.J. in a beard and bushy wig, but all I came up with was a big maybe.

"What's troubling you, Sammy?"

"Hmmm? Oh. Oh, nothing."

Hudson takes a bite of cake. "Well, then, what was the other question?"

"Oh. Right. I was just wondering…how much do you know about that guy who lives in your rental?"

"Bill?" Hudson shrugs. "He's a little unusual, but I think he's a decent fellow. Rommel seems to like him."

"What about the purse?"

"The one Rommel found?"

"Yeah."

"What are you driving at, Sammy?"

I take a deep breath and say, "I bumped into your renter at the mall. He was carrying all these packages. It was about an hour after someone broke into the Heavenly Hotel."

Hudson wipes up cake crumbs with the back of his fork and says, "You think *Bill's* the thief?"

"Well, Officer Borsch says all the crimes around here are connected. I mean, what was that purse doing in your trash can anyway?"

Hudson puts up a hand. "Hold on, young lady. First off, we don't know that the purse *was* in the trash can. Rommel might've found it just tossed over the fence. Second, Bill has no need to steal money. He has a well-paid job."

Just then Bill comes walking through the gate, wearing a windbreaker and baseball cap, as usual. He's carrying a briefcase and his nose is pointing straight down, as usual.

Hudson calls, "Evenin', Bill!"

Bill just pulls his ball cap and grunts, as usual.

When he's gone I whisper, "Who would ever want to hire *him?*"

Hudson chuckles. "Ah, Sammy. That's a good one. Who might you expect would hire a man like Bill Eckert?"

"I don't know...a place that needs an accountant?"

Hudson throws back his head and laughs. He shoos a moth from his boot and says, "My dear, things are not always what they appear."

"What do you mean?"

He looks out at the stars. "Ever listen to KRQK?"

"Sure."

"Have any favorite DJs?"

I shrug. "Marissa's crazy about Rockin' Rick."

Hudson smiles and hitches a thumb toward his garage. "Marissa's crazy about him."

My jaw about drops through the porch. "You're kidding! *He's* Rockin' Rick?"

"One and the same."

"No way."

He laughs. "Way."

"That's amazing!" I sit there for a minute, shaking my head, then I stand up and say, "I've got to get home. Grams is probably getting worried."

Hudson nods at the cookies. "So the lady likes shortbread." He looks at me and smiles. "With tea, I suppose?"

I laugh. "Exactly."

"I'll have to remember that."

"For the next time she comes over?"

One of his eyebrows arches up. "She told you about that?"

"Nope. I saw you myself. From the roof of the mall."

"Well I never." He leans forward and says, "Seriously?"

"Seriously."

Hudson wraps up a piece of cake and says, "Here. Give this to your grandmother and tell her I hope she'll stop by again soon."

So I run home, and before Grams can say anything about me taking so long I give her the piece of cake and say, "Hudson says hi and he hopes you'll stop by again soon."

"Cake?" She starts to take it, then says, "You go ahead. I prefer the shortbreads."

So I had a second piece of cake, and for the rest of the night Grams made me work on my knitting and purling. And you'd think time would go by real slowly, but it didn't. Knitting makes you think. Your fingers are busy pushing yarn around and pretty soon your brain starts wandering, looking for something else to do.

I thought about Hudson and Rockin' Rick and about things not being what they seem. And I thought about other people I know—like Mrs. Graybill and Officer Borsch—and wondered again why they were the way they were, and if maybe they had secret lives as *nice* people. I also thought about Gina and T.J., and what being *them* would be like.

But after a while I started thinking about having to go to school the next day, and what I was going to do about Heather Acosta. And the more I thought about Heather and her stupid Help Heal Heather Fund, the more I wanted to get back to school and straighten things out.

Trouble is, I didn't have a clue how.

SIXTEEN

The minute I got to school I could tell Heather'd been doing a lot of talking. While I'd been home putting knots in wool, she'd been busy burning up the phone lines, telling everyone what a monster I was. Kids would see me and stop to whisper to their friends, or point and cover their mouths.

And since Marissa hadn't shown up yet, I was walking around all by myself feeling really dumb. Then this brown-haired girl with studs and loops loading down her ears comes up with a couple of friends and says, "Heather happens to be my best friend, and if you ever touch her again . . ." She looks around a minute, thinking.

"What? You'll pin me down and machine-gun my earlobes?"

Just then Heather shows up.

Now Marissa had told me Heather's nose was taped up, but I guess I wasn't expecting to see what I saw because I took one look at her and busted up. I mean, she's standing there with ten hoops in her ears, and she's looking at me over the top of this enormous *cast* on her nose. It was so big I wanted to grab a pen and sign it.

But all that gauze and tape plastered on her face didn't stop her mouth from working. She gives me the evil eye and says, "C'mon, Tenille. Let's go before she breaks your nose, too."

129

So Heather and her groupie leave and I'm left standing there with the feeling that something's not quite right. When Marissa finally shows up I say, "Didn't your cousin break his nose once?"

She parks her bike. "Brandon? Yeah. Doing a back dive off the edge of our pool, remember? Why?"

"Did they tape up his nose?"

She shakes out her hair. "Yup."

I can see Heather at the tables, talking to Tenille. I nod in that direction and say, "Did it look anything like that?"

Marissa takes a look. "Wow! It's even bigger than it was yesterday! You must've really nailed her!"

The bell rings for homeroom, and while we're all standing there mumbling the Pledge my eyes shift over and stare at that mountain of tape on Heather's face. And pretty soon I'm wondering: what's gauze doing on her nose? I mean, if I broke it, I broke it on the *inside*. There's no reason to put gauze on the outside unless it's cut, and I know I didn't cut it.

Then I start thinking about how the tape on Brandon's nose had been smaller and kind of skin-colored. Heather's nose was buried in athletic tape, the white stuff they wrap your ankle with when you sprain it in sports.

Then it hits me. Her nose isn't broken at all. She's just putting on a show to get people to hate me. And it's working.

* * *

I hadn't missed much, being suspended. Miss Pilson was still talking to herself in Old English, Mr. Tiller was still moving X around the chalkboard, and Mr. Holgartner showed the second half of another video that had more static than socks on polyester pants. And when lunchtime finally rolled around I *still* hadn't figured out what I was going to do about Heather.

That is, until I heard her in the lunch line, standing a little too close to Danny Urbanski, telling him, "...and Dr. Gant says I can't take it off until Friday. It is *so* embarrassing! He says I really should be home taking it easy, but I just can't afford to miss that much school. That brat Samantha only got suspended for one day and I have to wear this all week. It's so unfair, don't you think?"

Marissa whispers, "Bro*ther!* Don't you just want to—"

"Pop her in the nose?" I say, and then we both laugh. Marissa won't admit it, but she's had a crush on Danny Urbanski for ages. A major crush. And watching Heather move in on him was steaming her potatoes.

She turns to me. "You're right, she's faking it. If only we could prove it!"

I go digging through my pockets and Marissa asks, "What are you looking for?"

"Some change." I pull out a few coins and give her a little smile. "I've got an idea...."

"What is it?"

"I don't know if it'll work but it's worth a shot. Stay here. I'll be right back!"

I found a pay phone right outside the office, and I got lucky—the girl using it was just hanging up. I hunted through the phone book until I found him in the yellow pages—Bertram Gant, MD.

By now my heart's beating like crazy so I take a deep

breath, pop in the coins, and say, "Hi, this is Heather Acosta," when someone answers the phone. "I came in a couple of days ago with a nosebleed?"

The receptionist says, "Oh, Heather. Yes, I remember."

"May I speak with Dr. Gant? Or maybe a nurse?"

"The doctor is in with a patient right now—let me pull your chart and see if one of the nurses can help you."

I say, "Okay," and let me tell you, my heart's beating in my ears and I'm having a lot of trouble breathing.

Finally a lady comes on the phone. "Hello, Heather, this is Mary. How can I help you?"

"Well, I was wondering if you could call the school for me."

"Call the school? Why?"

"Mr. Caan—our vice principal? He's making me wear a bandage on my nose."

There's a long silence on the other end of the phone and for a minute I thought I was wrong.

Finally she says, "A bandage? For a simple nosebleed? Why on earth...?"

Well, that's all I needed. I started sniffling like I was trying not to cry. "It's so embarrassing! He says I have to wear a bandage just in case it *was* broken or fractured or something. He says that if anything happens to it in P.E. he doesn't want the school to be liable or something. I don't understand it....All I know is that all the kids are making fun of me and I just want to die!"

Now Mary wants to get this straight. She takes a deep breath and says, "You're telling me that your principal—what is his name?"

"He's the vice principal—Mr. Caan."

"Mr. Caan insists that you wear a bandage on your nose because he doesn't want to be responsible if you get injured again?"

"That's right. He made me put gauze and tape over the whole thing and he says I can't take it off until Friday."

"*What?*"

"Can you please just call the school and talk to him? Tell him it's not broken and that I'm fine—that it was just a little nosebleed and I don't need to wear these stupid bandages?"

"I most certainly will!"

I look up the school's number real quick and give it to her. Then I hang up the phone and race back to the lunch line to find Marissa.

I grin at her and she whispers, "Where'd you go?"

Heather's only a few people ahead of us so I say, "I'll tell you when we're sitting down."

So we make it through the line and we're just about to sit down at a table when the loudspeaker blares, "Mr. Caan, please come to the office for a telephone call. Mr. Caan, to the office, please." I nudge Marissa and grin up at the loudspeaker and, she says, "What did you do?!"

So I tell her. And pretty soon she's got a hand in front of her mouth and we're both giggling and peeking over at Heather a few tables away.

A little while later, Mr. Caan comes steaming into the cafeteria. I kick Marissa under the table and say, "It's show time."

Now Mr. Caan was probably supposed to take Heather

to his office and straighten things out with her there, but he didn't. He found her and stood towering over her, yelling, "What do you think you're trying to pull? Take that ridiculous tape off your face right now!"

Heather sputters, "But Mr. Caan! The doctor says—"

Mr. Caan's looking like he's ready to kill her. "Yes, I *know* what the doctor says! I just had a very enlightening conversation with Dr. Gant. I've spent the last ten minutes listening to him read me the riot act about how *I've* been forcing you to wear a bandage on your nose. I ask you again, Miss Acosta, what are you trying to pull here? Why are you wearing that ridiculous bandage when all you had was a simple nosebleed?"

By now the entire cafeteria is quiet. And I mean *quiet*. No one's even breathing.

Heather turns as red as her hair. "But...but..."

"Take it off. Right now. All of it."

Pretty soon all the kids are whispering and moving in, trying to get a closer look at Heather peeling athletic tape off her face. And when all the tape's off her snotty little nose, Mr. Caan says very quietly, "Come with me."

I don't want to miss a minute of this so I say to Marissa, "Come on!" and we start following them outside.

But Heather forgot her purse, and when she goes racing back to her chair to get it, who does she see? Me.

All I do is give her a little smile. But it's enough to make her figure out that I had something to do with the trouble she's in. She comes after me saying, "You little—" and pretty soon she's all over me, trying to scratch my eyes out.

Mr. Caan comes racing back, and while he's trying to

pull her off me, Heather tries to punch me in the face.

It was probably the first punch she'd ever thrown—it just didn't have much experience behind it, if you know what I mean. Instead of coming straight at me, it came around from the side. And since I could see it coming a mile away, what do I do?

I duck.

And who does she hit?

Mr. Caan.

Now I don't think it hurt him too much, but I do think it was like poking an angry bear with a fishing pole. Mr. Caan practically drags Heather out of the cafeteria and pretty soon everyone's coming up to me, telling me "Way to go," and stuff like that.

Then Danny Urbanski says, "Hey! What happened to all that money they were collecting for Heather?" and that starts everyone else saying, "Hey, that's right! Where's my money! I want my money back!"

And there's Tenille, standing in the middle of the pack with her eyes darting around, looking for a way to escape the cafeteria before she gets mugged. But it's too late. Somebody sees her and calls, "Hey, Tenille! Get back here! We want our money! Where is it?"

Tenille's smile is as sweet as vinegar. "Heather has it— really!" Then she starts blubbering. "Oh come on, you guys...she made me do it! I didn't know! How was I supposed to know?"

I call over to her, "Oh yeah, right! I bet you want everybody to believe you didn't know she pricked me in the rear end with that stupid pin, either!"

Before Tenille can stop herself she says, "Oh, she told me *that*—she just never told me her nose wasn't broken! Honest!"

I give her a little smile and all of a sudden she realizes what she's done.

She says, "No, wait, I...That's not how it happened," but everyone's already shaking their heads and leaving.

Then Danny Urbanski comes up to me and says, "I'm glad you punched her. She deserved it."

Marissa grabs my arm. "Did you hear that? Can you believe it? Danny said he was glad you punched her." She pumps her hand in the air. "Yes!"

*　　*　　*

Kathleen Spencer was the office aide when Heather's mother showed up to have a meeting with Mr. Caan, and she said you could hear Mr. Caan's voice clear through his door and all the way down the hall. She also said that Heather spent the whole time before her mother showed up in the Box and that after the Acostas left the secretaries went crazy whispering about how Heather had been suspended for three days. They said that they couldn't remember anyone being suspended for three days, let alone a girl.

When I got back to homeroom at the end of the day, sure enough, Heather was missing. Marissa comes running up to me saying, "Have you heard?" and pretty soon *everyone's* running up to me saying, "Have you heard?" and telling me they never believed her in the first place.

136 Right.

On our way home from school Marissa says, "You want to get an ice cream?"

I say, "Sure!" and when we get near the mall she points and says, "There's Oscar!"

So we race across Broadway and when we get close we start slapping our feet on the sidewalk and making a bunch of noise. "Hi, Oscar!"

He stops and cups his ear, so Marissa calls, "Two Double Dynamos, please!"

He smiles and nods and pretty soon *chinga-chinga-chinga* he makes us change and we've got our drumsticks.

Now Marissa wants to sit right down in the grass and start on hers, but I say, "C'mon, I want to show you something."

So we take our cones and go inside the mall, and as I'm taking her up the escalator she says, "Where are we *going*?"

I just smile and lead her over to the "Employees Only" door; then I latch on to her wrist and drag her inside.

She whispers, "Sammy, no! What are you doing? Isn't this against the law or something?"

I keep on dragging. "C'mon, I know what I'm doing!"

That doesn't do much to convince her, but she comes along anyway. When we get to the door to the roof, she peeks around it like she's checking a stall in the girls' room. "Are you sure this is okay?"

I disappear around the corner and she comes charging after me. And when she gets on the roof her eyes bug out and she says, "Wow! This is *cool*."

I take her over to one side and say, "Look. You can see St. Mary's and the Salvation Army and..." and then I tell her about everything I'd seen when I was up here before and how you can see so much more with binoculars.

She says, "Check it *out*. You don't even need binoculars—this is awesome!"

So we run around the roof of the mall shouting at each other. "Look! Look!" until finally Marissa says, "I'll bet I can see my house from up here."

"I'll bet you can't. There are way too many trees in the way," which is true. East Jasmine is like buried in trees. They probably have enough trees there to start a forest.

She looks, but she can't see it and then all of a sudden she looks down at her drumstick and says, "Ooooh, yuck! This thing's melting all over me!"

Both our Double Dynamos are oozing out of their wrappers, dripping all over us. So we sit down and slurp like crazy until we've got them under control.

And we're sitting there, kind of roasting in the sun, licking away on our drumsticks, when Marissa says, "Do you think Danny's cute?"

I work on my drumstick some more. "Yeah, he's cute. But he ought to lose the ring."

Marissa sits up a bit. "Lose the ring? The ring's cool." Then she goes on and on about how him wearing his ring on the index finger of his left hand is so significant and how if he ever gave it to a girl it would mean something. And you can tell—she's spent hours thinking about Danny Urbanski's ring and why he wears it where he wears it and what it would mean if he gave it to *her*.

I laugh and say, "He only wears it on that finger 'cause

it fits there," and we spend another ten minutes talking about Danny Urbanski's ring.

Finally she takes the last bite of drumstick and says, "You don't *like* him, do you?"

"*Like* him? No!" I'd never even thought about liking him. I mean, I've known for a long time that Marissa liked him so what in the world would *I* be doing, liking him?

She laughs and gives me her trash. "Want to go down to the arcade for a few minutes?"

I think about the twelve cents I've got left in my pocket. "Nah—I'd better get home. I want to tell Grams about what happened with Heather today!"

So off we go, down the stairs, and when we get back into the mall Marissa goes one way and I go the other.

And I'm in the middle of putting our napkins and wrappers in the trash when a shiver runs down my back. I stand there a minute with my hands halfway in the trash can, then I pull the napkins back out and sit down, right there on the floor. And the longer I stare at the napkins the colder I feel, until finally my whole body is shivering.

I whisper, "No...it can't be," but Hudson's voice keeps echoing through my brain: "My dear, things are not always what they appear." And the more I think about it, the more I know.

I know who the hotel thief is.

SEVENTEEN

To prove it, I need money. Serious money. None of this twelve cents stuff.

I thought about running home and asking Grams, but I knew she wouldn't give me a bunch of money without me telling her why I needed it, and if I did tell her why I needed it, you can bet she wouldn't give it to me at all.

Then I remembered Brandon. I raced back down the corridor, dodging people left and right, and pretty soon I'm at the counter of Juicers panting, "Is Brandon here?"

The girl who's working says, "Yeah, hang on," and goes to get him.

Brandon pops out from the back room and smiles. "Hi, Sammy! What's up?"

I practically got down on my hands and knees. "I need to borrow some money—ten dollars? Twenty dollars? I promise I'll have it back to you tomorrow—maybe even today. Please?"

He checks his wallet. "I've got like four dollars on me. That's it. You're welcome to it, but that's all I can do."

My brain's racing. Four dollars is not going to do it. A five-dollar bill, maybe, but not four singles, no way. I lean as close to him as I can and whisper, "It's an emergency....Can you lend me some from the register?"

He whispers right back, "What are you, trying to get

me fired? No way I can do that." He straightens out. "Why don't you ask Marissa?"

"I would, only I don't know where she went!"

"If it's an emergency, why don't you have her paged?"

I blink at him for a minute, feeling really dopey; then off I go to have Marissa paged.

Only I never make it to the security office. I'm running down the mall, when all of a sudden right in front of me is Marissa. And standing next to her is Heather. That's right. Heather.

Now I should've gotten Marissa by herself and explained the whole thing to her, but I was in such a hurry I didn't. Instead I interrupt and say to Marissa, "I have to borrow some money—"

And I'm about to tell her it's an emergency when Heather starts laughing real mean. She crosses her arms and wobbles her head back and forth, saying, "'Sammy never asks me for money. Sammy wouldn't *think* about asking me for money....Sammy's my friend.'" She laughs some more, "Well, Marissa, I guess that shows you, doesn't it?"

Marissa looks at me like I've just punched her in the stomach. She digs in her pocket, pulls out a wad of money, and throws it at me. "Here, take the stupid money!" she says, then she runs off crying.

And I'm standing there feeling horrible, looking back and forth from the money on the ground to Marissa running toward the escalator, and I'm about to go chasing after her to explain everything when Heather reaches down and snags the wad of bills.

Well, there's no way I'm going to let Heather walk off with Marissa's money. No way. I say, "Hey! Give it back!"

She snickers. "You're dreaming." And she starts running away.

I don't care how much fun Heather Acosta's made of my high-tops, she was wishing for a pair right then. She saw me gaining on her, and I think her nose was starting to remember what happened the last time she tried to mess with me because all of a sudden her stupid grin disappears and she yells, "Help! Help!"

People are staring but that doesn't stop me. I chase her all the way to the escalator and tackle her so that she winds up with her face a little over the edge of the top step. I get on top of her, grab her hair, and say, "Give me Marissa's money!"

"No!"

I know I don't have much time before some security guard comes and hauls me off, so I push her face down toward the moving steps and say, "Give me Marissa's money!"

There go those steps, *thunk-kathunk-thunk-kathunk*, just skinning her nose, and all of a sudden she's very quiet.

I let her get a good whiff of the escalator and then I lean down and whisper, "I'd love to grind that snotty little nose of yours completely off, Heather. It's your choice — your nose or Marissa's money."

A second later her hand comes around and opens up. She chokes out, "Get off of me!"

I grab the money, step right over her, and go flying down the escalator. And when I turn around to look back, there are all these people standing around just *staring*. The whole escalator's practically surrounded by people with their mouths open.

I raced around looking for Marissa, but I couldn't find her so I ran outside and looked for her there. Still no Marissa.

What I probably should've done was call the police. Or at least go over to the station and tell them what I thought. Trouble is, they would've called in Officer Borsch and I would've been stuck talking myself blue in the face to someone who wasn't about to believe me. Not unless I could clobber him over the head with some proof.

And maybe I was crazy thinking I could prove who the thief was, but I had a plan. So I didn't go to the police station. I went straight to St. Mary's to get my proof.

St. Mary's Church is on a corner and has big bushes with yellow flowers along the sidewalk. And if you go up the brick walkway, there's a nice fat hedge around a statue of the Virgin Mary in the front courtyard. The hedge and the statue are up in this tall planter, so when you're walking into church, there's Mary, way up high, protected from kids scribbling on her legs by a nice fat hedge.

Between the hedge and the statue is the perfect hiding spot. You can sit right down on Mary's feet and have a real good view through the hedge of what's going on from the middle of Church Street, clear up and around the corner, halfway down School Street. And no one would ever think to look inside the hedge to see if somebody was there. I mean, it's *Mary's* spot, y'know?

About half a block from St. Mary's walkway I slowed

down and pulled Marissa's wad of money out of my pocket. There were three ones, a five, and a ten. I took the five and the ten and scribbled on them to mark them.

So I'm at the walkway, about to make a dash for the hedge, when Father Mayhew decides to take his dog for a walk. The last thing I need is for Father Mayhew to catch me camping out with Mary, so I just sit tight. Pretty soon the bell tower chimes and there goes Father Mayhew, around the corner and out of sight.

Then I see him—the hotel thief—turning onto Church Street, way down by the mall. I crouch down by the bushes along the sidewalk, keeping an eye on him as he gets closer and closer. Part of me's saying, Plant the money and hide! and part of me's saying, No, no. Wait until he's a little closer. And while they're battling back and forth, I'm just kind of frozen there behind those bushes feeling my heart beat faster and faster.

Then I hear a bike clicking along School Street. I look over my shoulder and can't believe my eyes. "Marissa!" I whisper as loud as I can.

She practically falls off her bike screeching to a stop. I put a finger up to my lips to stop her from saying anything, then I run over and make her get off her bike.

She says, "What are you *doing?*"

"Sssh! Come here!" I haul her bike back up the street and stash it behind some bushes.

"I was just on my way over to your apartment to tell you I was sorry for being such a jerk back at the mall."

"You weren't a jerk. I was being a moron! I should've gotten you away from Heather and explained."

"Well, what's going *on?*"

"Come on! I'll show you." I hurry her over to the statue; then I run toward the sidewalk and peek down Church Street. There he is, all right, about a block away.

I back up the brick walkway a little and put the ten-dollar bill down, face up, looking like a gift from God. Then I take a few steps back and put down the five. First I leave it wide open too, but I decide that's too obvious so I fold it in half and move it a little closer to the statue.

By now Marissa's doing the McKenze dance, biting a nail, dying to know what I'm doing with her money.

All I say is, "Quick! We've got to hide back here. Don't say a word!"

When Marissa sees that we're going diving in bushes she pulls back and says, "No way!"

"Come *on!*" I shoot her a you're-dead-if-you-don't look, and before you know it she's right there next to me, sitting on Mary's feet.

And when he reaches the walkway, my heart starts beating so loud that anyone coming by right then would've thought it was a miracle and the statue of Mary had come to life.

I whisper, "He's the hotel thief—I'm almost positive!"

"Who?"

I point to the end of the walkway. "Him!"

EIGHTEEN

Marissa looks at me like my marbles have just completely shattered. *"Oscar?* He can't be. He's blind!"

I just kind of smile and whisper, "How would a blind person know if his glasses were clean or not?"

She whispers, *"What?"*

"Sssh! Watch. Just watch."

Then it happens—Oscar stops.

Now he doesn't go racing over and snatch the money off the ground and *then* look around like anybody else would. He stops and stands there for a minute, thinking. Then, very slowly, like he's stretching his back, he moves his head from side to side, and backs his cart up a little to turn onto the walkway. Then he kneels down like he's going to tie his shoe, and when he stands back up the ten is gone.

I look at Marissa and she looks at me and we're both totally bug-eyed. Marissa mouths, *"Now* what?"

Well, I don't know, but I'm not going to tell her that. I just put my finger in front of my lips because the last thing I want is for ol' Oscar to find us. I go back to watching him, and sure enough, he's coming after the five. He moves forward a little, kneels down to tie his other shoe, and *whoosh*, there goes the five.

I look over at Marissa and that's when I notice it—the biggest, ugliest spider you'd ever want to see, climbing right up her sleeve.

She must've seen me looking at her arm because the next thing you know she *screams.* Then she jumps up, slaps at herself like crazy, and screams some more.

Who knows what happened to the spider. All I know is that Oscar the ice cream man was staring straight at Marissa, and when I stood up and looked at him, well, he knew right away that that money hadn't come from God.

And you'd think he'd just run away, but he didn't. He stood there, kind of looking over one shoulder, then the other. And that's when I realized that he wasn't about to just let us go.

Marissa's still screaming about the spider so I grab her by the shoulders and shake her. "Marissa! Stop it! Run to the police station. Now!"

I jump out from behind the hedge and I'm about to hop off the planter when Oscar grabs me by an ankle. Now this is no feeble grab—it's like a tourniquet around my leg. And any second he's going to yank me off the planter and I'm going to go *splat!* on the walkway, so I smack him with the sole of my other foot, right in the forehead.

His head goes flying back and his glasses fall off, and as I break free, sure enough, there's the face I saw through the binoculars. Only it's looking a whole lot madder than the last time I saw it.

I jump down and start running as fast as I can to the police station, but in the middle of running I realize that all Oscar has to do is get in a car and go, and no one'll ever find him. Then for the rest of my life I'll have to worry about where Oscar is and whether or not he's on the look-out for *me*.

So I circle back around to St. Mary's, and I sneak up to the courtyard, and what do I see? Nothing. He's gone, his glasses are gone, the cart's gone...there's no sign of him anywhere. Very carefully, I peek down Church Street. No ice cream man. Then I look down School Street. No ice cream man. I start running again, but now I'm not trying to get away from Oscar, I'm trying to find him.

So I head over to the mall, and I wind up running around it—the whole thing. And before you know it I'm cutting across the dirt where the new mall parking lot's going in, thinking that he's already gone and there's no way I'm ever going to catch him.

Then these kids come tearing by on their bikes, chasing each other through the dirt. I watch them go, and then I notice their bike tracks. I stand there studying the tracks, and suddenly I've got a good idea where Oscar might be.

So I start running again, but when I get to Maynard's Market I decide that what I've got to do is call the police. I tear up to the counter all panting and dying for air. "T.J.! Can I use your phone? Please! It's an emergency!"

He's holding the phone in one hand and lighting a cigarette with the other. "Can't you see I'm using it?"

"*Please!* It's a matter of life and death."

He blows smoke out his nose like a dragon. "This ain't a public phone—now beat it!"

I slap the counter. "Then *you* call! Dial 911 and tell

them the hotel thief's on the corner of Broadway and Wesler!"

"What?"

I yell, "Call them! Now!" and then race out the door.

I just *knew* there had to be a shortcut, so instead of running clear down to Wesler Street I turned down an alley. That was a mistake. It's not like I've never been down an alley before. I've been down plenty of alleys—just none quite as scary as this one. The ground was slimy, like the sun never really got a chance to dry it out, and there were old metal garbage cans that smelled like sewage and were buzzing with flies.

And I was slipping along the dirt, trying to stay up on the edge where the ground was a little bit drier, when this gigantic dog comes charging up to the fence, snapping and growling and barking, trying to crash through the pickets.

My heart was already pumping pretty good, but the second that dog popped up it exploded. I jumped back, slipped, and landed flat in the mud. I tried to calm myself down, but really, all I wanted was to get out of there.

I knew I was close because I could see the back of the Heavenly Hotel. So I decided to climb the wall. And it probably wouldn't have been that hard, only my high-tops were caked with mud and I kept slipping. By now there's a whole chorus of dogs barking up and down the alley, sounding like they're all going to break out at the same time and eat me alive, and I'm really starting to panic.

I look around real fast and roll one of those stinky garbage cans over to the wall and then flip it upside down.

I climb on top of it and look over the wall and there's the old pepper tree, bent over, all by itself in the middle of the empty lot. Trouble is, I can't see past the tree's branches to tell if he's there or not.

So I climb over the wall and circle around the back side of the tree as quietly as I can. My heart's going a million miles an hour and I'm barely breathing, and when I peek past the branches what I see is a man with long blond hair and a goatee, hunched over an ice cream cart, looking in a mirror.

It's Oscar, all right. And in his new disguise I *did* recognize him, only not as the ice cream man or the hotel thief, but as the guy who'd stopped to talk to André the day Marissa and I had gone to see Gina.

He starts changing his shirt, and that's when I decide that I don't need to see any more. What I need is the police.

Trouble is, as I stepped away from the tree I snapped a twig and the newly blond ice cream man freezes with his shirt half off. Then he looks over his shoulder, right through the branches, right at me.

For a second we both just stared at each other, but then he took a quick look around and came charging after me.

I wasn't about to try any more shortcuts. No way! I ran straight to Wesler Street and headed toward Broadway with ol' Blondie right behind me. And when I got down to Broadway I turned the corner and nearly crashed into a lady with three lavender poodles coming out of the Pup Parlor. I danced around them and tangled them up pretty good, so by the time Oscar got there they were going every which way, trying to knock him to the ground.

I raced across the street, dodging cars and jamming traffic, but when I looked over my shoulder, he was still after me and gaining.

Now I'm heading for the police station by way of the mall because I figure if I can make it to the mall, Oscar'll stop chasing me. There are just too many people at the mall. And since the fastest way to the mall is through the parking structure, I decide to cut through that.

So I go charging up this grassy slope between the sidewalk and the parking lot, but the sprinklers must have been on earlier because the grass is all wet and I wind up slipping and falling.

Oscar's charging at me, only about fifty feet away. And there's the side entrance to the mall, straight through the parking structure, about a hundred and fifty feet away. I scramble back to my feet but it's easy to see—I'm never going to make it.

I run down the hill and into the parking lot, calling, "Help!" as I work my way between cars. But I don't see anybody, and then I remember how many people had come to Heather's rescue when I'd tackled her by the escalator: Zero. So I quit calling for help and started looking for a place to hide.

First I crouched behind one car, then another. But no matter where I moved I was still exposed on three sides. Then I saw a Dumpster in a corner against a wall, so I crawled over and squeezed behind it.

And I've just crouched down, hugging my knees real

close, when Oscar runs by. And I'm about to breathe a sigh of relief when I hear him stop and come walking back.

My heart's already slamming against my chest and my lips are all dry and there's sweat dripping down my face, but I practically turn inside out when I hear a noise inside the Dumpster.

The noise happens again, and that's when I realize there's something inside the Dumpster. Something alive. Oscar hears it too, because he walks right up to the Dumpster, looks in the top, and laughs. "You're history, girl."

I hold real still and watch his feet go back and forth along the ground. Then it happens again—that *noise*. Oscar leans over and gets halfway inside, looking for me.

Leaning on the wall right above me is the Dumpster lid. And I know it's heavy because I've lifted one before—just a few inches to throw trash away. And there's Oscar, digging through the Dumpster saying, "Where are you, you little brat? I know you're in here!" So I take a deep breath, stand up, and yank down on the lid as hard as I can. And when the lid clanks closed, Oscar's pinned inside with his legs sticking out.

Cuss words start echoing around inside that Dumpster, and even though I'm holding the lid down as hard as I can, I know that any second he's going to bust loose.

Giving up would've been like trying to get away from an angry yellow jacket—it's just not something you can do, even in high-tops. You're better off just staying where you are and trying to swat it down. So I pull myself up on top of the Dumpster and sit on the edge. But Oscar bucks around even harder and you can tell—he's going to be able to push the lid open, even with me on it.

So I stand up on the lid and start jumping up and down like a jackhammer. The lid's clanging like crazy and I'm yelling, "Help! Help! Somebody, help!"

And I'm up there for what feels like *days*, bouncing on the Dumpster, yelling at the top of my lungs, hearing the ice cream man spew out words I didn't even know *existed*, when who comes charging around the corner?

The Borsch-man.

I never thought there'd come a day when I'd be happy to see Officer Borsch, but let me tell you, I don't think I've ever been so relieved to see anyone in my whole life. He takes one look at me bouncing on the Dumpster, puts a hand on his holster, and says, "Come off of there."

I sit down and start to slide off the front when Marissa comes running around the corner with Tall 'n' Skinny. She yells, "Sammy!" Then when she sees what's going on she starts jumping up and down. "You caught him! You caught him!"

Officer Borsch tells Tall 'n' Skinny, "Chad, get the lid." He motions Marissa and me back. "Move back...now!"

We back up, all right. About two inches. And we watch Tall 'n' Skinny prop up the lid while Officer Borsch stands back with his feet spread and his gun drawn. And Oscar's in the middle of pulling himself out of the Dumpster when a mangy orange alley cat comes streaking across his back and hits the ground running.

When Oscar gets out, he's looking like the Man from Planet Slime. His wig's all crooked and has spaghetti and lettuce smashed in it, his back is covered with dirt and rust from the lid, and there's a tea bag dangling from one shoulder.

Officer Borsch shouts, "Spread your hands out against the wall! Move it!" then comes in from behind and kicks Oscar's ankles apart. And while Tall 'n' Skinny frisks him, Officer Borsch hollers out his rights and before you know it Oscar the ice cream man is wrapped up in handcuffs and on his way to jail.

And Marissa and I are coming along for the ride.

NINETEEN

The first thing Tall 'n' Skinny wanted to do was call "our" parents. Marissa was quick: "They're gone for a few days on business."

Tall 'n' Skinny frowned. "Do you have a number where you can reach them?"

"Uh, no. They usually just call in at night."

"Don't they have a pager?"

Marissa shook her head.

"Hmmm."

You could tell he was going to keep asking questions until he found a way to talk to somebody, so I asked, "Would you like me to call my grandmother?"

He tugged on his mustache and nodded. "I think that would be a good idea."

So I called Grams and gave her a rough sketch of what was going on. Then I handed Tall 'n' Skinny the phone and while he was talking to her, I discovered that Tall 'n' Skinny has a name. It's Sergeant Jacobson. I kind of uncovered the nameplate on his desk. I also found a picture of his daughter, who's probably just a little younger than I am. In the picture she's holding this snake and it looks like she's about to use it as a jump rope.

Anyhow, after Sergeant Jacobson got off the phone, he brought us sodas and then opened up this big tin of

M&Ms and said, "Help yourself." Then he made some phone calls and pretty soon he says to us, "They'll have that ice cream cart picked up shortly, and we've got a team at the Heavenly now, questioning the manager."

After that, he starts filling out a bunch of forms. When he gets to the part about how come Marissa and I have different last names when we're sisters, well, I'm sweating it out pretty good. I kind of look down and say, "My mom ran off when I was pretty young. I'm Marissa's foster sister." He didn't ask me any more questions about it so I guess he believed me, and I didn't feel bad about lying because it's not that far from the truth.

Then he asks to hear the story. The whole story. He even wants to hear the part he'd already heard that first night at the Heavenly Hotel. So I tell him, and when I get to the part about going on the roof of the mall and how I'd seen Oscar sitting all by himself, buffing his glasses, he says, "You were on the roof of the mall?"

Marissa looks at me like, I told you it was against the law! but I just nod and tell Sergeant Jacobson how I hadn't thought anything of Oscar buffing his glasses at the time, but that later I started thinking that it's just not something a blind man would worry about doing.

"You could see him cleaning his glasses from the roof of the mall?"

"Through binoculars, sir."

He shakes his head and laughs. "Those binoculars again." Then he says, "I should start carrying a pair. Of course I've never even thought to go up on the mall roof. . . ."

Marissa kind of wiggles in her seat. "I've been up there too! It's really cool. You can see everything!"

Sergeant Jacobson tugs on his mustache a little. "Did you see all this through binoculars, too?"

I jump in and say, "Oh no, sir. I saw that before. Marissa went up with me today, and that's when I figured out where the napkins came from."

"The napkins?"

"You know, the Double Dynamo napkins? Like the one we found at the Heavenly Hotel?"

"What napkin did you find at the Heavenly Hotel?"

Well, I'm figuring out in a hurry that Marissa didn't have time to tell him anything about napkins, and that Officer Borsch never said a word about it, either. "You know—the napkin with the writing on it? The one that matched the napkin that was left under Mrs. Graybill's door?"

He throws up his hands. "What? Wait a minute. Slow down." He leans forward and asks, "What note?"

Now let me tell you, in my stomach there's this giggle that's just dying to get out. I slap it down and say, "Didn't Officer Borsch tell you any of this?"

"Noooo…."

I shake my head. "I guess he really *did* think I was making it all up. I mean, he said he thought I'd forged it, but I figured maybe he was just in a bad mood."

Sergeant Jacobson's eyes pinch closed and he leans back in his chair like all of a sudden he's got a splitting headache. "And *why* would Officer Borsch think you'd forged it? What was written on the napkin?"

"HH four twenty-three. You know—Heavenly Hotel, room four twenty-three. Gina's room?"

He nods. "All right... and why did Officer Borsch think you'd forged it?"

So I tell him about the note that was left under Mrs. Graybill's door and how Mrs. Graybill thought I had written it. Then I tell him how when I'd found the napkin rolled up on the hotel fire escape I'd given it to Officer Borsch right away to prove that the thief had left the note under Mrs. Graybill's door.

Sergeant Jacobson twists a few hairs of his mustache. "And Officer Borsch didn't believe you?"

I shake my head. "No, sir. Like I said, he accused me of writing both notes."

He bites the inside of his cheek for a minute, then says, "Will you excuse me? I'll be right back."

Well, he's not leaving to shake more creamer in his coffee. He's off to have a little chat with Officer Borsch. And while he's gone Marissa and I dig into those M&Ms. You wouldn't believe how many we ate. By the time Sergeant Jacobson came back we'd chomped down so many that even Mikey would've been proud.

Sergeant Jacobson has the napkins with him and he flattens them out on his desk. "Just from looking at it right now, I'd say the handwriting matches." He flips them over. "And they're both Double Dynamos." He looks at me. "So you noticed the napkins matched and you noticed him cleaning his glasses—was there anything else?"

"Well, yes, sir. Sort of. See, Gina had told us that she had been talking with some friend of hers out in front of Maynard's. She didn't know her friend was in town and she wound up telling her where she was staying and how she had to go to the bank to start an account because she didn't like carrying around so much money. She told me she didn't remember anyone listening to their conversation, but you don't think of Oscar as being an eavesdropper. I mean, everybody knows he's blind and almost deaf. He's always bending his ear and acting like he wants you to speak up, so that's what everyone does. And when he's around, people don't quit talking about whatever they're talking about—they just figure he can't hear them anyway.

"So I started thinking—all these burglaries are happening in the same vicinity. Maybe Oscar just cruises around watching and listening to people all day and when he finds out someone's going on vacation or going to be gone, well, *chinga-chinga-chinga* he just goes in and makes himself some quick cash. I think that's probably what happened to Gina."

Sergeant Jacobson chews on this a minute. "But when did you know it was him?"

So I tell him about planting the money and how Oscar had scooped it up, and then Marissa says, "You know, that money was mine. Do you think I can get it back?"

Sergeant Jacobson nods, then lets out a sigh. "But I'm afraid there will be some red tape."

"Why?"

"Because I imagine a lot of people will be putting in claims for any money we recover, and there's no way to prove whose is whose."

I smile at him. "Marissa's money will be easy to spot."

"Oh?"

"I marked it."

"You *did?*"

I nod, and they both say, "Well?"

"I wrote 'I'm the hotel thief' on both of the bills. It's tiny, but it's there."

Sergeant Jacobson throws back his head and laughs. "Well, that's certainly another nail in the man's coffin!" Then he adds, "His name's not Oscar, by the way. It's Larry Daniels, and his probation officer from South County's been looking for him."

That makes my eyes bug out a little. "Yeah?"

"He's not somebody I would recommend tackling without backup." He shakes his head at me. "You've got a lot of bubbles in your soda, young lady."

Just then his phone rings. He snatches it off the hook. "Jacobson here." He says a lot of "Uh-huh"s and "Good"s, and pretty soon he says, "Excellent!" and gets off the phone.

He smiles at us and says, "They've got Mr. Daniels' friend from the Heavenly in custody."

"André?"

"No, no. André's a good man, very cooperative. I'm talking about the man that Mr. Daniels visited." Then he adds, "André knows our Mr. Daniels as Lew."

Marissa shakes her head. "So Oscar's really *three* people?"

Sergeant Jacobson nods. "The way I piece it together, Daniels would wear the blond wig when he walked around town, a different one when he was on a job, and then the fishing hat and glasses when he was playing Oscar."

"So who was the guy he visited at the Heavenly?"

"Apparently he's quite a lowlife himself—long history of lawbreaking and overnighters at the jail house. I don't think we'll have any problem getting information out of him, although we might not need it. They've found quite a bit of incriminating evidence in that ice cream cart."

I lean forward. "Like . . . ?"

"A few disguises—one was a brown wig and beard and some black gloves. There was also a stash of cash and a few items of jewelry, including a silver-plated watch."

"Is it Gina's?"

"Sounds like it. Suns and moons on the wristband—"

"That's it!"

Marissa says, "But wait a minute, Sammy. How'd you know he'd be under that big tree?"

"Remember how you laughed at me because those bike tracks didn't go anywhere? Well, I was chasing around looking for Oscar when these bikes came whipping by me through the dirt. And after I saw *their* tracks, I knew that the tracks under the tree couldn't have been made by bikes. They were spaced too regular . . . too *even*. Like they'd been made by a giant tricycle or something."

Marissa says, "Like the ice cream cart."

"Right!"

When Sergeant Jacobson finally gets everything documented, he shakes our hands and says, "Can I give you girls a lift home?"

Well, I don't want to have to walk all the way home from East Jasmine so I say, "No, that's okay."

He walks us to the front door, and just as we're going down the walkway, Gina comes sailing up in purple and silver scarves. "Hey," she calls to me, "I just heard!" She plants a great big kiss on my cheek. "I can't believe you caught the guy!" She holds me out in front of her and says, "You know what I'm going to do? I'm going to do your birth chart, that's what I'm going to do. I'll even progress it for you!" Then, before I can say, No really, that's okay, she gives me a hug and runs up the station steps. "Gotta go I.D. my watch and see about my money!"

We watch her swoop into the police station and then kind of shake our heads and laugh. Finally Marissa says, "I've got to go get my bike."

So we head to St. Mary's, and once we get her bike we sit on the curb for a long time and talk. First about Oscar and everything that had happened, then about people not being what they seem. And when Marissa says, "Yeah, but Oscar's just one guy! Most people are exactly what they seem," I break it to her about Rockin' Rick. And when her jaw gets back into socket about *that*, I ask her whether she thinks Mrs. Graybill or Officer Borsch could have secret lives as nice people. She just laughs and says, "If Rockin' Rick looks like a dork, then *anything's* possible!"

"What about Heather Acosta?"

"Oooh…" she says. "I take it back!"

We both laugh about that, and then Marissa asks, "You want to come over and spend the night?"

I think about it a minute. "Nah, I want to get home to Grams."

And I do, even though I know Grams is going to keep me up all night. First she'll want to hear the whole story. From the top. Then she'll want to hear it *again*. Then she'll pull out her boots and my knitting and while I'm sitting there, tangling up wool, she'll blame everything on the binoculars and make me promise never to use them again.

A promise she knows I just can't keep.

Wendelin Van Draanen is a computer science instructor, a wife, a mom, a runner of dogs, and a part-time singer in a rock band. She also rises at five o'clock each morning to write funny stories about smart, determined young women. Ms. Van Draanen lives in Santa Maria, California, where she is currently at work on a new mystery starring Sammy Keyes.

sammy keyes

AND THE skeleton man

by Wendelin Van Draanen

What does Frankenstein have that a skeleton wants?

Sounds like a bad Halloween joke. But Sammy Keyes isn't laughing. She's the one who collided with the skeleton while he was making his getaway. And she's the one who discovered Frankenstein tied to a chair with his head twisted around. Someone's taken "trick or treat" *way* too far.

When Sammy tries to puzzle out what really happened Halloween night, she's amazed at how many people have something to hide—and how far they'll go to keep their disguises intact.

Of course, Sammy's got a few secrets herself. And more than a few tricks up her sleeve. She'll need them all to unravel this tale of greed and grudges and getting even…

And coming soon:
SAMMY KEYES AND THE SISTERS OF MERCY